HEAD OVER HEELS

There he was. Naked. Nude. Standing with the bed conveniently blocking his lower half.

"Let's go," Jess hissed. She was practically hyperventilating.

So was I.

I heard a weird squeak come out of Jess but I didn't dare take my eyes off the movie screen. I grabbed my purse and moved toward the aisle, keeping my eyes on the hottest hottie ever. The guy sitting on the end of the back row was moving his head back and forth trying to see around me.

"Sorry," I whispered as I turned to go.

The next thing I knew I was falling. I threw my hands out. My foot slid off my flip-flop and my body did this weird twisty movement and the next thing I knew I had landed face-down.

In some guy's lap.

Obsessing
Orlando

KASSY TAYLER

SMOOCH NEW YORK CITY

Thanks to Kate for letting me play.
Dedicated to Kassy, Tayler and my niece Beth Ann.

SMOOCH ®

December 2005

Published by

Dorchester Publishing Co., Inc.
200 Madison Avenue
New York, NY 10016

ISBN 0-8439-5603-8

Printed in the United States of America.

Visit us on the web at www.smoochya.com.

Obsessing Orlando

Chapter One

I . . . can't . . . breathe.

My Vera Bradley tote bag hit the floor as I looked around my room in shock. I kept a close hold on my pillow, not that the pillow in itself was that important to me, but the pillowcase was covered with a picture of Orlando Bloom. Shirtless. You can find almost anything on eBay. You just have to know where to look.

"Did your boyfriend leave you?" my brother Justin asked sarcastically as he dropped my suitcase by the door and sauntered off to his room across the hall. I didn't even bother making a face at him—I was trying to catch my breath.

"Jenna." My mom came up behind me and placed her arm on my shoulder. "Do you like it?"

I looked at the fresh lime-green paint on the walls. I looked at the new pink and yellow quilt and the pile of coordinating pillows on my bed. I looked at the bright pink bean bag chair behind a curtain of . . . beads? At least my computer and my desk had been spared the attack of Pepto-Bismol.

1

"Where's all my Orlando stuff?" I asked. I think I was suffering from shock. The entire room looked liked something off of *Trading Spaces*. I was definitely having trouble breathing.

"It's all right here, sweetheart." My mom was always calling everyone "sweetheart" or "darling" or "honey." I didn't feel like being her sweetheart. I didn't feel sweet at all. I felt . . . violated. I had only been gone for a week and she had come in and re-decorated my room. Wasn't I entitled to an opinion on the subject? Shouldn't I have had a say on what went on my walls? It had taken me forever to get everything the way I wanted it. I had the posters fixed so that the last thing I saw when I fell asleep at night was Orlando. I could even look in the mirror on my vanity and see him looking back at me—smiling at me with his sexy smile and his dark brown eyes and those cheekbones. . . .

My mom opened the door to my walk-in closet to show me a stack of posters and pictures lying on the floor.

"*Ahhh!*" I screamed. "Are they stuck together?" I ran to my closet to rescue my treasures.

"I promise I was very careful," my mom said in her *patient* voice. I hated her patient voice. It always meant that I was about to hear something that I didn't like.

"However"—I braced myself for what was coming—"since your walls look so nice I would appreciate it if you didn't mark them up with tape and tacks. After all, we paid a lot of money to have this done for you. As a surprise. You're going to be *fourteen* soon. Don't you think your room should look like it belongs to a freshman in high school?"

Wow! The full barrel. She had got me with the money guilt *and* the coming maturity issue all in one shot. My mom had never really approved of what she thought was an unhealthy obsession with Orlando Bloom. She just didn't understand. He was special. He was different than the rest of those guys that girls had crushes on like Justin Timberlake and Chad Michael Murray. I could see it in his eyes. He was waiting for me. To grow up. To be his special . . . love. Forever.

I had only been in the door for five minutes and I already had my mom ticked off at me. I had better "tread lightly," as my dad liked to say.

"Would it be okay if I hung them in here?" I asked in what I hoped was a humble voice. Sometimes my mom had problems with my *tone*.

"Sure."

"Mom?" I asked.

She looked at me expectantly.

"The room looks nice. I really like it."

"Thank you," she said. "Your dad had to run to the office and we're going to go out to eat as soon as he gets back. Bring your laundry down so I can get started on it."

"Okay."

She still wasn't happy with me, but at least I had done the right thing. There would be no lecture later

3

about expressing gratitude for the sacrifices my parents made and being a responsible young adult and stuff like that.

I waited until she was gone before I made a dive for my cell phone. I fell into the bright pink bean bag as I pushed speed dial button number four. Number one was the house of course, number two my mom's cell, number three my dad's and four belonged to my best friend. My brother, Justin, was number five, in case I needed a ride or something like that.

"Jess!" I moaned in my best dramatic voice when she answered her cell. Jessica Gilbert was my best friend. She had been since sixth grade when we both realized that our computer skills teacher was insane. Her family had just moved to town and my friends from elementary school had all been placed with a different teaching team than me since I was what the teachers considered "academically gifted." Basically what it meant was that everyone in the AG classes had more homework than everyone else. In seventh and eighth grade we had both made the volleyball team and we were both trying out for the JV team at our high school the next week. I was a hitter, since I had grown about eight inches between seventh and eighth grade. Jess was a setter. We worked well together.

"Jenn!" she said. "What's wrong?"

"Are you home yet?" I had just spent a week with Jess's family at a cabin they had rented on the lake. It had been boring. No Internet, no DVD player and no cute guys over the age of twelve. Jess's little brother,

Hunter, had future cuteness potential. He'd have to give up being a pest, though. And grow a foot or two. He had also brought a friend with him and they had spent their week catching frogs and snakes to scare us. We had retaliated by stealing their clothes when they were skinny-dipping. They said we did it just because we wanted to see their . . . thingies. . . .

Gross.

"We just got home, Jenn." She sounded like she was out of breath. "The new neighbors moved in while we were gone."

"And?" I waited patiently. I knew my news was much more important than something as trivial as new neighbors.

"Mrs. Gladden said they have a son our age." Mrs. Gladden was Jess's neighbor on the other side. She had been old ever since I knew her, and she used to babysit for Jess and Hunter while their parents were at work. Jess had declared herself too old to need a babysitter in seventh grade, but Mrs. Gladden still looked after Hunter until last summer when he turned eleven. Now she just fed their cat and got the mail while they were on vacation. In return Hunter cut her grass.

I waited for Jessica's announcement.

"A cute son."

"According to your nosy neighbor?" I said. "The one who thinks Harrison Ford is a hottie?"

"Yeah," Jess laughed. "He was kind of hot in *Star Wars*."

"That movie is ancient!" I laughed with her as I

looked around my room. It still seemed foreign and I wondered if my stash of Starburst had survived my mom's purge.

"So have you seen him yet?" I asked as I played with the beads that hung from the ceiling. They hit against each other with a clacking sound as they swayed back and forth.

"No. She said he's trying out for the football team and that he's running all the time. What is that noise?"

"Beads. They hang from the ceiling."

My brother Justin played football. Varsity. He was going to be a junior but he had been on varsity since halfway through the season his freshman year. He was a defensive end and already had colleges looking at him. My dad sure was proud of him. He was president of the Athletic Boosters and always stopped by the school on his way home from work to watch practices and talk football with the rest of the dads. He expected me to make the volleyball team. Carry on the tradition, he said. Jess and I had both spent a week at the coach's volleyball camp and we had played AAU last spring. I thought our chances were pretty good.

I had more important things than volleyball on my mind at the moment. Like Orlando.

"Beads? What beads?" Jess asked.

"The pink and green beads that form some sort of curtain, I guess, around this pink bean bag chair. My mom redecorated my room."

"A pink bean bag? Awesome. I think. What's the rest of it look like?"

"It's all bright green and pink with a new quilt with big squares on it." Now for the critical, life changing announcement. "Jess, she took down all my posters." I waited for my words to sink in.

"Omigosh." Jess always ran her words together when she got excited. I never had any trouble understanding her but sometimes my mom and dad did. I usually had to translate for them.

I knew that Jess would understand. One wall of her room looked like a shrine to Tom Welling. You know, the guy who plays Clark Kent on *Smallville*. He isn't much of a publicity hound and pics of him are kind of hard to come by. Plus he is married, which is kind of gross, I guess.

Ew. What if Orlando got married? He was kind of serious about that Kate Bosworth. Oh well, it's not like I really expected him to wait around while I grew up. Just as long as he is available when I did get there. Anyway . . .

Jess also had a wall devoted to Daniel Radcliffe, the *Harry Potter* guy. We had sat through the third movie at least five times. He was pretty cute, but he wasn't Orlando.

"So what are you going to do?" she asked. I could hear noises in the background.

"She said I could hang them in my closet."

"You'll never get to see him!" Jess exclaimed, somewhat breathlessly.

"What are you doing?" I asked.

"Changing clothes."

"Are you going somewhere?"

"Dad told Hunter to cut the grass and I'm going to do the trimming," she explained.

"Oh."

What she really meant was that she was going to hang out in the front yard and wait for the new neighbor to come by.

"So do you want to go see *it?*" I asked. *It* being Orli's latest blockbuster. Rumor had it that he got naked. I wasn't going to miss that.

"Your mom isn't going to let you see an R-rated movie." Jess knew what I was talking about. I'd been obsessing about this movie all week.

"She doesn't have to know." We had already had this discussion several times at the lake.

"You mean sneak in?"

"Yes." She knew that's what I meant. Why was she playing dumb?

"My dad would kill me."

"Come on," I urged. "We'll just tell them we're going to see *Harry Potter* again."

"Wouldn't you rather see Tobey Maguire's latest?"

Tobey Maguire was kind of cute. Especially in those movies like *Spider-Man* where he took off his shirt.

"No." The decision was made. It had been made a long time ago when Orlando had been cast as the dashing hero yet again. He was so great in those historical roles. Like when he played Paris in *Troy*. I had even forced myself to read the *Iliad*. And that was after I had read *Lord of the Rings* and *The Simarillion*. My dad thought I was a genius or something since I had even walked to the library and checked those books out. It's not like Justin would have driven me. He wouldn't be caught dead near a library unless there was a cute girl involved.

"I've got to see him."

"Ohmigosh," Jess interrupted me. "Igottagocallyoulaterbye."

She hung up on me!

Over some random guy.

I wonder what he looks like.

Chapter Two

Did I mention that I look like an elf? Not the Keebler kind. *The Lord of the Rings* kind. Jess had decided that everyone is either an elf, a hobbit or a human. She even categorizes some people as Orcs. Those kind are usually really disgusting and mean. Just like the Orcs. Anyway, I'm definitely an elf because I'm tall.

I hate being tall. I'm already as tall as Orlando and taller than most everyone in my class except for a few of the basketball players. I have light brown hair that's about halfway down my back and hazel eyes. I hate having hazel eyes. It's not the color that's bad, it's just the name of it. Couldn't they come up with something more clever than hazel? Who thinks up these things anyway?

I guess I look a lot like my brother and we both look like a mix of my mom and dad. Except my mom's eyes are blue. I wish I had her eyes. They can look right through you, especially when you've done something stupid. It's just like she's wearing those contact lenses like Orlando wore when he played Legolas. They were cool, but I really like him better with his own brown eyes. They're so . . .

"Still Legolusting?" my brother asked.

"Shut up," I said and closed the screen on my computer. Yes, I had been looking at a fan site.

"Dad's home. Mom said to come on."

"Whatever." I posted my away message and grabbed my purse.

Mom and Justin were already arguing about who was driving. Justin wanted to take his own car so he could leave when he got bored. Mom wanted a family dinner so she told him he had to ride with us. Our Boxer, Ellie, looked between the two of them as they went back and forth. Mom won. After all, my parents were the ones paying for the gas. Justin didn't have time to work a real job since he was always going to football camps and stuff. He helped my dad out at his construction sites when he had time, which didn't happen very often.

Dad walked in right in the middle of it. He ignored them as usual. Mom and Justin were always getting into it. Dad said it was because they were so much alike.

"So how was the lake?" he asked. He gave my shoulder a squeeze as he opened the refrigerator.

"It was okay," I sighed.

"Boring, huh?"

"David. We're going to eat," my mom said. "Get out of the fridge."

Dad emerged with a piece of cheese and ignored my mom. "Things will get busy soon enough and you'll wish you were back there doing nothing."

Yeah. Right.

"Is everyone ready?" Dad asked like he had been waiting on us instead of the other way around.

We piled into our SUV and panic set in as the garage door closed.

"Wait!" I said. "I forgot my cell phone." I was digging around in my purse hoping it would show up but I knew I had left it by the bean bag.

The car kept moving.

"Jenna, you can live without it for an hour," my mom said, once again using her *patient voice*. She didn't even look at me, which was a good thing since I was making a horrible face and was having trouble breathing again.

"Ha ha," Justin snickered and waved his phone at me.

"Turn yours off, Justin," my mom said.

"Ha ha," I said back at him as he shoved his cell in the pocket of his cargo shorts.

My dad looked at us in the rearview mirror with his hazel eyes.

Hazel. What a stupid name for a color.

Everyone loves my dad. Jess thinks he's hot. Gross. Maybe he is. He's not fat or anything. He goes to the Y every morning and works out and still has all his hair. Mom says he's a tall Russell Crowe, which I guess is good. I liked *Gladiator* and it's one of Justin's favorite movies.

Jess thinks Justin is hot too. She practically has a meltdown whenever she's over and he has his shirt off. I think he takes it off on purpose when she comes to the house. I have to admit that Justin is built, but *ewwww,* he's my brother.

Jess says we're an entire family of elves and hers is nothing but humans with hobbit hair. Jess's hair is blonde, thick and kind of wavy. She has blue eyes too. You can put a lot of adjectives in front of blue to make them sound cool. There's not much you can do with hazel.

We went into O'Charleys and had to wait, of course. It was Saturday night and everyone in town was there. We snagged a table in the bar and ordered some über nachos. Mom and I got Diet Cokes, Dad and Justin, water with lemon. They were into healthy eating, although I wouldn't consider nachos healthy.

"Coach Robbins called me today," Dad announced as he picked up a chip dripping with chili and cheese.

Coach Robbins was the head football coach at our high school. I zoned out and started checking out the tables to see if there was anyone there I knew, or wanted to know. I had already heard more than I wanted to about play-action coverage and interceptions.

"Whadhesay?" Justin asked as he chewed. He must have gotten a banana pepper in his sauce because he grabbed his water and took a gulp. I had already picked about three out of mine. I can't stand them.

My mom smiled and waved at somebody she knew, then elbowed my dad. He looked around and waved, then went back to the more important subject of football.

"Apparently there's a new player that's just moved to town," he said. "A quarterback."

I started paying attention. They had to be talking about Jess's new neighbor.

"We've already got one," Justin said. His best friend Ryan was the quarterback. "What grade is he in?"

"Sophomore," Dad said.

"Then he'll be on JV," Justin replied, as if it was a done deal.

"Coach Robbins said this kid was really good. He played varsity as a freshman."

"Where at?" Justin asked. I could tell he was getting pissed. He was in love with the fact that he was the only one we knew who had played varsity as a freshman.

"Kenton."

"Kenton," Justin snorted. "They're double-A. We're a four-A school. Ain't no way."

"I'm just telling you what Coach Robbins said," my dad explained. "I guess we'll all find out next week when you start practicing."

"Did you talk to Richard?" my mom asked. Richard is Ryan's dad. He always hangs out with my dad and talks about football like it's their religion or something. They were already planning on Justin and Ryan going to State together and then playing professional football. They had the next two seasons planned out and there wasn't any room on their team for a new quarterback. Unless he was going to be on JV and they could compare him to Ryan or something like that.

"I called him," my dad said. "He's going to do an Internet search on him."

"What's his name?" I asked, trying to sound nonchalant.

"Will Addison."

"What do you care?" Justin asked me.

"Justin," my mom warned. We all knew he was just ticked off because he couldn't call Ryan and trash this guy.

And for some reason I already felt sorry for Will Addison. We had lived in the same town my entire life, so I didn't know what it was like to have to go to school where you didn't know anybody. Jess had said it was scary when she started middle school but once we became friends everything had been fine. This Will Addison guy was coming in as a sophomore from a really small school where he probably knew everyone, and the coolest guys in his new school, meaning Justin and Ryan, were already going to hate him. And they'd get everyone else to hate him too, just because he might be a threat to Ryan's position on the team.

And I thought I had it rough.

Our blinky thingy went off and we went to the lobby so we could be taken to our table. Jess's family came in just as the hostess picked up our silverware and menus. Like I said, everyone in town was there.

"Why didn't you answer your cell?" Jess said as she grabbed my arm.

"I left it at home."

My parents were yakking with Jess's while the hostess kept a patient smile on her face. Justin was impressing Hunter by making the muscles in his arms jump. He always keeps the sleeves on his polos pushed up so everyone can see how big his muscles are.

"I saw him," she announced dramatically. Or as dramatically as you can when you're whispering.

"Will Addison?"

"How do you know his name?"

"My dad knows everything that goes on in this town."

Jess stole a look at my dad and then at Justin, who gave her one of his flirty smiles. I wanted to smack him.

"So?" I hissed, bringing her back to the issue at hand.

"Look." She held up her phone and showed me a picture. It was blurry. Obviously she had taken it when he ran by her house. "He waved at me," she said. "He's definitely an elf." She already had him categorized. She was excited and her hand was moving so I grabbed it so I could look at the picture.

I couldn't tell how tall he was because it was mostly a profile of his face. He looked like he was cut, but not as big as Justin. It was more like he was lean, kind of like Orlando. His hair was dark and messy and the ends curled up around his ears, but it might have been because he was all sweaty from running.

"I can't tell," I said. "Is he cute?"

Jessica almost fainted. "Yeah, he's cute."

"Who's cute?" Justin asked. He reached for the phone. I tried to get it from Jess but she was putty in his hands. He looked at the picture and then flipped the screen shut. "Looks like a pussy to me," he said.

"Justin!" My mom rolled her eyes. She is so PC. It was all a show for Jess's parents. Did I mention that her dad was the pastor at our church?

"I think our table is ready," Dad said.

Yeah Dad, for about an hour now.

"Call me," I said to Jess as I trailed after my family. It was too bad we had just spent the week together or I would have asked to sleep over at her house. I wanted to see this Will Addison for myself.

Chapter Three

I didn't have any trouble talking Justin into taking me and Jess to the movies the next afternoon. It was raining and he was bored and afraid Mom would make him clean out his drawers or something. She always made us clean out our drawers and closets before she took us shopping for school clothes, but today she had her nose buried in a book while Dad and Ellie had hit the couch to watch a baseball game.

We had gone to the early service at church and Jess and I had sat in the front row of the balcony to see if Will Addison's family came in. Her parents had gone over to meet his and had invited them to church, of course. No pressure there. No need to come just because the pastor is your next door neighbor. They didn't show, but they could still come for the late service. Jess had to sit through both of them. Sometimes I felt sorry for her. Being a PK (Pastor's Kid) wasn't the greatest thing but her parents were pretty cool about movies and clothes. Not that either of us dressed like hoochies or anything like that.

Anyway, we passed notes written on our bulletins and she finally agreed to sneak into the movie, but I think it was mostly because her dad kept looking up at us while the choir was singing and she was afraid we'd get into trouble for disrupting the service, not that we actually were.

Justin called Ryan and we went to pick him up first so they could get a look at Will. Jess told me at church that she hadn't seen him since he ran by, but since it had started raining while we were at dinner last night that didn't surprise me. She also said that his house had gotten a pizza delivery late that night and his parents had told hers that they were still trying to get unpacked and stuff. Jess's upstairs bedroom luckily happened to be on the Addison's side of the house.

We picked up Ryan, which meant I had to get into the backseat of Justin's Wrangler. This wasn't easy because my legs are long and Justin and Ryan both push the front seats back as far as they will go since both of them are over six feet tall. I had to sit all scrunched up and get thumped by Justin's bass, which was under the seat, while they yelled at each other over the CD that was playing. Why didn't they just turn it down so they could hear each other instead of yelling? Guys are so stupid sometimes. Anyway, Jess came running out as soon as Justin pulled into her driveway.

"He just left," she reported to Justin like she was part of their conspiracy to check out Will Addison. Justin was all scrunched up against the steering wheel while trying to hold the seat up with his left hand.

Why didn't he just get out so she could get in? He was being stupid, so I shoved the seat against his back and held it, pinning him against the wheel while pulling Jess in by her arm. I shoved harder when I heard him grunt. I'd probably pay for it later, not that he'd admit that I had caused him any pain.

Jeeps look cool when you're riding in them, more so with the top down. But in reality they aren't that user-friendly. Especially if you've got to climb into the back while wearing a skirt, which Jess was doing.

She was so obvious. Duh. As if my brother would even look at a freshman.

"He must have his permit," Jess added when she was finally settled. I saw her looking into the rearview mirror trying to catch Justin's eyes or something. "He was driving and his mom was with him. There was another guy in the back."

"Thanks for the report, spy girl," Ryan said sarcastically. He was the youngest of three and thought he could dump on us like his older sisters had on him. Jess made a face at him. She had lots of experience with pesky younger brothers.

"So what are you guys going to see?" I asked again, just to make sure Justin wouldn't screw up our plans.

"That Vin Diesel movie."

"I think Vin Diesel is gross," Jess said.

"Are you crazy?" Ryan turned around to look at her. "He is the bomb."

I didn't care much one way or the other. Besides, I knew Jess liked Vin Diesel. Well, maybe not Vin so much as his arms. She was just trying to get the guys to talk to her. I thought Paul Walker was pretty cute in *The Fast and the Furious* and I had seen *XXX* because it was one that Justin watched a lot.

"What are you guys seeing?" Ryan asked.

"Either Tobey Maguire or Daniel Radcliffe."

"Again?" Ryan sputtered like he was my dad or something. "How many times are you guys going to watch those movies?"

"As many times as it takes," I said in my sweet voice.

Jess gave me a look. I felt pretty proud of myself for misleading the guys. I was feeling pretty cool about the whole "sneaking into an R-rated movie" thing.

Our cinema complex had twelve theatres. Six to the right and six to the left. All we had to do was pick whichever movie was showing on the same side as Orlando's and we were set. Have I mentioned that the entire rating system is stupid? How many teenagers are going to watch movies with their parents? And most parents don't have time to go to the movies like teenagers do. Why don't they just let us bring a permission slip or something like that? Really. They should think about all the money they're losing because of their stupid rating system. We're just going to watch the movie when it comes out on DVD anyway. Except for me. I couldn't wait. I had to see Orlando. I had read some stuff over the Internet about his role and there was some scene where you could supposedly see pretty far south, if you know what I mean.

My cheeks were burning just thinking about it.

We were in luck. It turned out that Tobey Maguire's movie was showing on two screens. One on both sides. We got our tickets and took off towards the left. Justin and Ryan turned right. They had started to ignore us as soon as we got out of the Jeep, which was fine with me since they liked to embarrass me and Jess whenever they had a chance.

Just last summer Jess and I had been at the mall talking to a couple of cute guys and Justin and Ryan came up and started talking to us. I should have known better, but I thought the guys might think that I was cool, too, since I had such a cool older brother. Anyway, Ryan had asked Jess if her feminine infection had cleared up and then Justin dumped a cup of ice on my head. The guys we were talking to laughed and I screamed at Justin. I had to call Mom to come and pick us up and Justin had wisely spent the night at Ryan's. I had even heard my mom and dad laughing about it later that night when they thought I was asleep.

Brothers could be such a pain sometimes. Justin hadn't done anything like that in a while, but that didn't mean that he wouldn't if given a chance. I was happy that they were ignoring us, but Jess wasn't. She was even pouting as we went down the hall towards the movie, which was all the way on the end.

I took a quick glance over my shoulder and saw that the ushers weren't paying attention. I pulled Jess into the alcove, where I knew Orlando was waiting just inside.

"What?" she asked as I peered around the door-way to look at the ushers again.

"This is it," I hissed.

"Oh," she said. "I didn't think we were really going to do it."

I rolled my eyes in the most dramatic way I could and grabbed her arm. I pulled her into the theater.

They were pretty far into the coming attractions phase, which was just how I wanted it. Everyone was concentrating on the screen. There were two guys sitting in the back row on the end, so I dragged Jess into the next to the back row and moved to the middle seats. A couple came in and sat on the other end of our row. The theater was only about a third of the way full since the movie had been showing for a while. We slumped down low in the seats and kept our feet on the floor so the ushers wouldn't have an excuse to yell at us when they did their power-tripping sweep of the theater. I hate it when they do that. They always act as if you're pulling the stuffing out of the chairs or something when you prop your feet up. They should be more worried about what people are putting on the floor. My shoes actually got stuck one time because I had to sit over a spilled drink. Gross.

We had just got settled when the movie started. *I can't breathe!* There he was. Orlando. Screen god. My future husband.

I was already thinking up a pretty good fantasy to get me to sleep that night. Me and Orli. Maybe I should pretend I was the one playing his leading lady.

23

Me, Jenna Wheeler, movie star, cast as Orlando's girl-friend. What a start. And on the set Orlando and I fall in love. I will have awesome dreams tonight.

Oh cool, there's a close-up of his face. I wish Jess would quit being so hyper. She's ruining the movie. She keeps twisting around like the FBI is after her or something.

I love his eyes. They are so . . . dreamy. And his voice . . .

"Ohmigosh," Jess hissed.

"What?"

"It's Mrs. Gladden," she whispered as she shrunk in her seat.

I looked and I couldn't believe it. Mrs. Gladden had just walked in and sat down about two rows in front of us. What was she doing here? Ew. Gross. Don't tell me she had the hots for Orlando.

"We gotta go." Jess was practically moaning.

"Shhh." I kept my eyes on the screen.

Jess crawled over me and did some weird hunched over walk towards the aisle.

I—can't—breathe. There he was. Naked. Nude. Standing there with the bed conveniently blocking his . . . er . . . thingie.

"Let's go," Jess hissed. She was practically hyper-ventilating.

So was I.

I heard a weird squeak come out of Jess but I didn't dare take my eyes off the screen.

Where did she go? I was going to kill her.

I grabbed my purse and moved towards the aisle,

keeping my eyes on the screen. I wondered if I could get a copy of that shot on eBay. As if I could get that by my mom.

I got to the aisle and turned towards the exit. The guy sitting on the end of the back row was moving his head back and forth trying to see around me.

"Sorry," I whispered as I turned to go.

The next thing I knew I was falling. I threw my hands out. My foot slid off my flip-flop and my body did this weird twisty movement and the next thing I knew I had landed face down.

In some guy's lap.

I—can't—breathe. I'm really serious this time. I couldn't. My purse strap had got hung up on the cup holder behind me and I was wedged between the seat and some guy's long legs, with my arm kind of pinned behind me.

The guy tried to climb out from under me and his friend started laughing. I managed to wiggle away and fall out into the aisle.

I saw some heads turn around to look at me.

God please let the floor open up and swallow me now.

"Are you okay?" the guy asked. He was standing by now and he grabbed my arm and hauled me up. Somehow I had lost my flip-flop and I was reaching for it when he yanked on my arm.

"Wow, you're tall," he said when I finally staggered to my feet.

Yeah, and you're observant.

His eyes were dark, or at least they looked dark

with the lights being out and all. His hair was dark and kind of flipped up on the ends around his ears. His face even looked dark, like he was sunburned or something.

"Shhhh!" Somebody hissed.

I hated it when people told me how tall I was. Like I didn't already know. I slid my foot into my flip-flop.

"Yeah," I mumbled. "Thanks."

"Great line, dufus," the other guy said. I heard the impact of a fist on skin and then someone said *"ow,"* but I couldn't tell which one.

I couldn't run out of there fast enough. I could hear the guy and his friend laughing as I went out the door.

"I can't believe both my neighbors were in there," Jess said as soon as I fell through the door.

"What do you mean *both* neighbors?" I asked. I looked around the doorjamb for ushers. No one was watching so we ran down the hall towards the Tobey Maguire movie.

"Mrs. Gladden," she said. "And Will Addison."

I stopped dead in my tracks.

"Where was Will Addison?" I asked. I already knew the answer.

"Behind us. On the end."

I. Can't. Breathe.

Chapter Four

Over the next few days I spent a lot of time hanging out with Orlando, trying to forget that I hadn't even entered high school yet, and I'd already made a complete fool of myself in front of a supposedly cute upperclassman. I cleaned out my closet enough to free up one entire wall for my posters. Of course, I had to slide some up behind the shelf but I had a pretty good collage going on the wall. I dragged the bean bag in there, along with a lamp, set my iPod to Maroon Five and was able to forget for a little while the most embarrassing thing that had ever happened to me.

I still couldn't believe that I had fallen face first into Will Addison's lap. I was also living in fear that Jessica would tell Justin about it. She always got so goofy whenever he was around. Justin would get a good laugh about it, probably make fun of me for the rest of my life and report to Mom that I had snuck into an R-rated movie. She would just love hearing about that.

To make matters worse, I still wasn't really sure what Will Addison looked like. Jess kept describing him as dreamy, but I hadn't gotten a good look at him since it was dark. It's kind of hard to see what someone looks like when your face is slammed against their jeans.

How was I supposed to avoid him when school started? It would be easy for him to figure out who I was since I was so tall, according to him. I could just hear him now.

"Hey, aren't you the tall girl that fell face first into my lap?"

I could just die. I would be known as the "tall girl" for the rest of my life. My mom had even griped about my height when we went shopping for school clothes. Our school had a dress code. Skirts and shorts had to be longer than your arms held at your sides and no bare midriffs. But my arms and legs were so long, along with the rest of my body, that it was hard to find stuff that fit without making me look like a total dork.

It just wasn't fair. Jessica had gotten all kinds of cool things to wear. I wish we could wear the same clothes and then we could trade outfits and stuff.

At least I had a big closet to *not* put my new school clothes in. All Jess had was a teeny one as wide as her door. My dad was a builder, so we had a really cool house with lots of neat extra details like built-in cabinets and our own personal bathrooms. He had taken over the business from his dad, who had retired and now lived in this really awesome cabin on the other side of the lake from where I had been with Jessica. The "rich side" was what Jessica's mom had called it when I pointed out where they lived. These days my grandfather built wooden furniture and my grandma painted pictures and sculpted with pottery.

At the moment, Mom, Dad, Justin and I were all piled into the car, on our way to their place for the weekend. Since my grandma's birthday is just a few days before mine, we always did some sort of celebration together. I loved visiting them. The cabin always smelled like Christmas and everyone helped cook the meals. Then we'd all watch movies together or work puzzles although Justin thought it was getting kind of lame. He's so selfish, all he thinks about is *his* life and how *he's* so worried that *he* might be bored or that there was something better going on somewhere else.

I wished I could tell Gran about falling on Will Addison, but my mom would ask all kinds of questions and then I'd have to lie so it was just better if I didn't mention it.

Gran would think it was funny. She always thought things were funny and loved to laugh. Dad said she used to do some modeling when she was young and was always the life of the party.

I guess I look like her since I'm tall and have hazel eyes. Maybe Gran knew a better name for it than hazel. I'd have to ask her this weekend.

Justin had whined about missing a Friday night with his friends chasing girls, so we left early on Saturday morning. I would have preferred to drive up on Friday night and slept in on Saturday, but Justin got his way as usual. He'd slept the entire way and I'd read a book called *Putting Boys on the Ledge* about some girl named Blueberry. I thought it would be cool to have an original name like that, but the girl in the book thought it was weird. Isn't it funny how even people with cool stuff aren't happy about it? I was just wondering if anyone would think it was cool to fall face first into the lap of a cute guy when we finally arrived.

The weather wasn't as hot at the lake. Gran had lots of pots and planters on their deck that over-looked the lake. They were filled with flowers of every color along with ferns and ivy. They had a big choco-late lab named Tucker. We had brought Ellie and both dogs took off down towards the water. They had a new kitten, too, a Siamese with big blue eyes.

"What's his name?" I asked when I saw him.

"Frodo," she said.

"Because his eyes look like Elijah Wood's?"

"Uh huh," Gran said and gave me my special smile. I think Gran understands me better than anyone, ex-cept maybe Jess.

Grandpa, Dad and Justin went down to look at the water as if it had changed or something since they'd been here and Frodo went back to chasing around the flower pots. Dad waved at Mom. He wanted to show her something, so she went down the steps to the pier.

"Let's get lunch on the table while they're poking around," Gran said. "I got some new dishes."

"Again?" I asked. It seemed like she had new dishes every time we came.

30

"They are my weakness," Gran confessed. "I love setting a pretty table. I think it's like a piece of art." We looked at the dining room table, which was all co-ordinated with matching napkins and had a big arrangement of flowers in the middle. It looked nice and special.

"It will get trashed pretty quickly," I said. My brother eats like he's starving all the time.

"They might act like they don't appreciate it," Gran said as we walked into the kitchen. "But they'd miss it."

I knew I would. I felt fairly confident that Gran would like the present we had picked out for her. It was a hand-painted pitcher that my mom had found at a craft fair. Gran always said that her most prized possessions were a set of plates that Justin and I had made at some paint-it-yourself pottery store. We had decorated the dishes with our names and handprints. I hadn't even started kindergarten when we had done them. They hung on a plate rack beside the bar, where everyone who came in could see them.

Gran had fixed my favorite—chicken casserole and deviled eggs. She gave me a bowl of strawberries to clean and slice while she placed some of those frozen dinner rolls on a pan to bake.

"Gran?" I asked.

She stopped what she was doing to look at me.

"Do you like having hazel eyes?"

"It's kind of late to worry about that now," she laughed. Her eyes crinkled up but I noticed that they looked kind of sparkly behind her dark lashes. I guess she still wore mascara. And she had to be at least sixty-five but didn't look it. Not compared to some of the other grandmothers I had met. "Why do you ask?" She looked at me again like she was laughing at some secret. "You're not thinking about having an eye transplant, are you?"

"Gran," I said in my most dramatic voice. "As if Mom would let me do that, even if it was possible. She won't even let me get tinted contacts."

"Why would you want to? It's not as if you need glasses—or has something changed since I saw you last?"

"Nope. Still twenty-twenty. Just had them checked."

"Good. So what's the problem with having hazel eyes?"

"They're boring. And the name is stupid."

Gran titled her head as if she were thinking about what I said. Then she started nodding as if she agreed with me. "You're right. Hazel is a stupid name for a color. I wonder who even thought of it. But the color isn't boring."

"It's not?'

"Nope. According to your grandfather it's a very exciting color. He always says he can tell what kind of mood I'm in by the color of my eyes."

"But they're always the same color!"

"No, they're not. Sometimes they're green, sometimes they're gold and sometimes they're kind of grayish."

"Really?"

"It just depends on how I'm feeling."

"So what color are mine now?" I asked.

Gran leaned in real close and looked at my eyes. I looked back at her and saw that hers were kind of green around the outside and gray around the dark part in the middle.

"Green mostly," she announced. "You must be happy."

"Yours are too," I said.

"See!" Gran gave me a hug. "They're always the greenest when my grandbabies are around,"

"We're not babies anymore."

"You'll always be my grandbabies. No matter how big you get."

We went back to fixing lunch while I thought about the eye thing. I'd have to start paying attention to see if they changed colors.

Gran was pretty smart. I bet she could help me figure out how not to die of embarrassment the next time I saw Will Addison.

"Gran?" I decided to ask her.

She closed the oven door and turned around at the exact same time that my stupid brother came clomping through the door.

"I'm starving," he announced like it was world news or something.

"Have a piece of fruit," Gran said and gave him a hug. "I wonder if I fixed enough to feed you."

"We can always send out for pizza," Justin teased her.

I knew what he was up to acting all charming. Even though it was my birthday, he'd wind up going home with some cash. Gran and Grandpa were always handing us twenty dollar bills.

We had lunch and then went for a walk around the lake so we could look at all the new houses being built while Grandpa and Dad talked about construction stuff. We watched a movie and then it was time for dinner. We had steaks on the grill and then Mom carried out a cake with sparklers on it for Gran and me to blow out and took a bunch of pictures of us with the sparklers going.

We gave Gran her pitcher and she loved it. Then Grandpa made a big production about carrying out this long thing as tall as me, covered up with a sheet.

"Ta da," he said and jerked off the sheet.

I can't breathe!

It was a life-sized cutout of Legolas. His eyes were really blue and cool-looking and hanging off his quiver of never ending arrows was a Vera Bradley gym bag with my initials on it.

With a matching cosmetic bag.

And a hundred dollar bill inside.

I let out a big squeal and Tucker and Ellie thought it came from the lake and took off barking, which got them out of our way since they'd been begging for steak. I threw my arms around Grandpa and Gran.

"I love it!"

"Legolas was my idea," Gran said.

"She shops online all the time now," Grandpa said. "The Internet's the worst thing that ever happened to my bank account."

"Watch out or I'll start surfing the shopping channels," Gran said.

Did I mention that I'm the same height as Orlando? It was really cool to stand right next to him. I could almost pretend that it really *was* him.

I did later when I was up in my half of the loft. Justin was still downstairs watching TV. I had gone to bed early. I couldn't wait to get Orlando to myself. I stood him at the end of my bed and just looked at him. Then I rolled up against my pillow and looked at the pillowcase.

Sometimes when I was pretending, or "fantasizing" as my mom called it, it was almost as if Orlando were really there. We were in our own cabin on a lake, hiding from the paparazzi while he was in between movies. He was always so sweet and honorable and we'd talk about our wedding day. He was going to wait for me to get out of school and then we'd have a wonderful life together.

That night I dreamed about school. I couldn't find my locker. I couldn't remember my combination. I had totally missed volleyball tryouts and all I was wearing was my underwear. Worse yet, they were tighty-whiteys instead of Victoria's Secret.

And Will Addison was laughing at me.

Chapter Five

Football practice started the same week as volleyball tryouts. Justin was doing what he called two-a-days and seemed to be in a perpetual bad mood. We tip-toed around him for the most part. He could be really moody and snappy when he wanted to and no one wanted to be responsible for making him blow up.

Dad said it was because he was tired from practice. Mom said his testosterone levels were up.

Gross.

I just figured it was because Will Addison was good and it ticked him off.

Since Justin was in such a funk Mom decided not to bother him with taking me to tryouts. She worked out a schedule with Jessica's mom that got us there and back for a week.

Jess and I were pretty confident that we'd make JV. I was definitely the tallest one trying out and Jess was pretty solid on the back row and with her setting. It would have been nice to make varsity because the coach was pretty cute, even if he was pushing thirty.

The JV coach had just graduated from college and thought she was pretty hot, Jess and I decided after our first day. She seemed more interested in flirting with the varsity coach than watching us and teaching us skills and stuff. The varsity girls didn't like her much because they were all in love with the coach.

You can learn a lot by hanging out in the stalls in the restroom and we were pretty much invisible anyway, being incoming freshmen and all, so it wasn't too hard to figure out the scoop. Some of the varsity girls did get kind of friendly when they realized I was Justin's sister. Jess got pretty mad about it, but I told her that I thought they were all a bunch of phonies and she felt better. They even had a little birthday party for me after tryouts were done for the day, which was kind of sweet. Even if it was just a cupcake from the convenience store close to the school.

That night we went to dinner, without Justin since he was at practice. Jess gave me a *Life Story* magazine that was all about Orlando, which was pretty cool, and my mom and dad gave me a new wallet to match the tote that Gran had got me. They said that my new bedroom was my real present, which was cool, I guess. It wasn't what I would have picked out since all my pics had been banished, but I was trying really hard to be fourteen and act all mature and stuff. I didn't realize that being fourteen would be so busy.

On the night before cuts a bad storm blew up. It was a hot day and we were all sweating in the gym and got pretty excited when the thunder started because we knew it would cool things down.

We heard the football team as they ran inside the building. They could practice in the rain, but not if there was lightning outside, which there was. Some of them stuck their heads in the gym and whistled and stuff. I made a face at Justin and Ryan when they looked in. I couldn't believe it when they waved back. Of course, they could have been waving at the varsity girls who were all smiling and posing for them.

Sometimes Justin could be cool when he wanted to be.

"I wish they'd let us go too," Jess whispered to me. The coaches were explaining what would happen with the cuts.

I knew she was just hoping we could get a ride home with Justin instead of her mother.

We sat there for what seemed like forever and they finally dismissed us. It had gotten pretty dark outside and it was pouring.

The older girls all ran squealing for their cars. Some of the football players were still hanging around in the parking lot and I watched as a couple of girls squeezed into the back of Justin's Jeep.

The rest of us had to wait for our rides to pull up to the gym door and run out and jump in. Jessica's mom had left a message on Jess's cell saying she was running late. She had to pick up Hunter and his friend from soccer and decided to get them first since they didn't have any shelter from the storm.

The coaches waited around with us so they could lock up the gym. We could tell the JV coach was real upset about having to hang around.

Anyway, I got into the middle row of the van and Jess got in the front seat. Hunter and his friend were all the way in the back and talking about some video game, so I ignored them. We were on our way out of the parking lot when Jess's mom slammed on the brakes.

"Isn't that our neighbor?" she said.

We looked to where she was pointing and saw a boy standing under the shelter at the front of the school. He was soaking wet and his dark hair was plastered to his head. He looked like he was shivering and he kept jumping up and down like he was trying to stay warm. All he was wearing was one of those sleeveless Underarmor shirts and a pair of shorts.

Jess turned and looked at me with a big grin on her face.

I can't breathe.

"Yeah," she said. "I think it is."

I made a face at her.

"Well, we just can't leave him here by himself," Jessica's mom said. "What's his name again?'

"Will Addison," Jess said.

How could she? She knew I had fallen on him at the movie. She knew he was the last person I wanted to see. I hadn't even been over to her house since it happened out of fear of running into him.

I shook my head *no* as Jessica's mom swung the car into the drive in front of the school.

"Hi, Will," Jessica's mom said in her friendly voice. She had rolled the window down and the rain was spraying in. I also noticed that the wipers were smacking Will with rain as he came over to the van. "I'm your next door neighbor, Mrs. Gilbert."

"Hello, ma'am," he said.

"Do you need a ride?"

"My mom's supposed to get me, but she didn't know about practice being let out," he explained.

"Have you called her?"

"My battery was dead on my cell so I didn't bring it."

"Get in and we'll call her and tell her you have a ride," Mrs. Gilbert said.

"That's okay ma'am, I can wait."

Yes! I tried not to let my relief show.

"It's no problem to drive you. Come on, you're getting soaked."

Noooooooooo!

I watched as Will looked around the deserted parking lot. If anything, it started raining harder and I was getting wet from the spray coming through the open window.

"I guess it's a good idea. Thanks, ma'am," he said.

Geez he was polite.

He ran around the front of the van and slid the door open. Hunter and his friend were on the edge of their seat, as if royalty had just climbed into the van.

I thought he smelled like a wet dog.

"Hunter," Mrs. Gilbert said. "Look and see if there's a towel behind you."

Hunter leaned over the seat, pulled out a towel and handed it to Will.

I kept my face turned towards the window.

"Have you met my daughter yet?" Mrs. Gilbert

asked. She was watching Will through the rearview mirror as she drove out of the parking lot. "This is Jessica and that's Hunter back there and his friend Daniel and this is Jenna Wheeler."

"Hi," he said, kind of shy-like.

"Hi," I mumbled back, still looking out the window. I could sort of see his reflection and watched as he mopped off his hair with the towel. It was long and dark and hung over his ears and his eyes since it was wet. He pushed it off to the side and dried his face and arms.

The van got sort of steamy and smelly and Mrs. Gilbert turned the air up. Jess started pushing the buttons on the radio since it had been on the contemporary Christian station.

I knew she was trying to impress Will.

"So how do you like living here?" Mrs. Gilbert asked.

I was pretty sure Will just wanted to be left alone.

"I kind of miss my friends," Will said.

That surprised me. The normal polite answer would have been "I like it just fine."

"I'm sure you'll make some new ones when school starts," Mrs. Gilbert said.

Not if Justin had anything to do with it.

"Yeah, you can hang out with the football players," Hunter said.

Get real, Hunter. You don't have a clue.

"And you already know the prettiest girls in the freshman class," Mrs. Gilbert added.

"*Mom,*" Jessica moaned.

He was looking at me. I could see his eyes reflected in the window.

"What grade are you in?" Mrs. Gilbert asked.

"I'm a sophomore, ma'am," Will said.

"Then you should have your driver's license soon?"

"Yes ma'am."

He sounded kind of funny when he said that.

We were taking Daniel home first instead of me like I'd hoped and I still had to deal with the fact that I'd have to climb over top of Will when we got to my house. At least the conversation had stopped and I could keep my face plastered to the window without looking too rude.

I did notice that Mrs. Gilbert kept looking at me through the rearview window.

"Jenn," Daniel said when we got to his house. "I think my backpack is under your seat."

I wanted to kill him. Why hadn't he got it out before he climbed into the back? Boys are just so stupid.

I had to pull it out and it weighed a ton. Daniel just stood there waiting in the rain. It seemed to take forever for me to wrestle the bag free. Total embarassment. Then I had to turn and hand it to him. It was either that or drop it in Will Addison's lap.

I wasn't going there again. No way.

Wow. Will's eyes were really brown. Big and brown with really long, dark lashes. I tried to look away before he could see my face, but his eyes were so nice.

And then he smiled at me.

A really nice smile with dimples and white teeth and everything.

"Hey, I know who you are," he said. "I thought you looked familiar."

Jess straightened in her seat.

I felt my breath catch in my throat.

"You're the girl from the movie. The one with the Legolas guy."

"Nope, never seen it." Was that my voice?

"Yeah, I know," he said with his perfect smile. "You left before it was over." He looked at Jess. "You too."

"Hey Mom!" Hunter yelled from the backseat. "I thought Jess wasn't allowed to see R-rated movies. That movie was R-rated, wasn't it?"

Mrs. Gilbert looked at Jess and then looked at me in the rearview mirror.

"She's not," she said. I knew that voice. My mom had the same one. We were dead.

Chapter Six

I stood in the rain on the sidewalk in front of my house and watched the van drive away. Will had tried to tell me he was sorry as soon as he realized that he had told on us, but I had ignored him, practically tripping over his long legs as I climbed out of the van. Besides, it's easy to ignore someone when all they're doing is mouthing words at you. I hope he got the message. Geez. Talk about clueless.

I had ten minutes left to enjoy life and then I was dead because I knew Mrs. Gilbert would call my mom as soon as she got home.

Or else Mr. and Mrs. Gilbert would have a long talk with Jess about making mature decisions and hanging out with the right people and then she would call my mom. Either way I was dead.

As I ran up the walk I tried to decide which was worse. Having your dad at home a lot so you got the yelling out of the way or having to wait for him to get home at night.

Oh great, my dad was already home. His truck was

sitting in the driveway. Hard to build houses when it's pouring rain.

Maybe I should just go ahead and tell them. Get it over with. Maybe I'd get some points for confessing.

Not likely. My mom would have a field day with this! She'd get to talk about me growing up and taking on more responsibility and building trust. The same old thing she had said over and over again to Justin. *Puhleeze.*

Maybe they wouldn't find out. Maybe Jess's parents would think it wasn't such a big deal. Maybe they would think that it wasn't any of their business what I did. All they had to worry about was Jess.

But Jessica's dad was also our pastor and he was supposed to be our moral compass or something like that.

I was pretty much dead.

I could hear my mom and dad in the kitchen as I came in through the laundry room. I knew mom would be mad enough at me without adding tracking mud through the house to my crimes. They were both laughing about something. At least they were in a good mood.

I decided that a hot shower would make me feel better and give me time to figure things out, so I went straight up to my room and jumped into the shower. I opened the door and kept leaning out, so I could listen for the phone to ring.

So far, so good.

I wrapped up in a towel, put another one on my head and found my mom standing in my room with her cell phone in one hand and a pillowcase in the other.

My Orlando pillowcase.

The one where he's shirtless.

I . . .

"Jenna," she said. "Carla Gilbert just called me."

Can't . . .

"Did you and Jessica sneak into an R-rated movie?"

Breathe . . .

"Yes ma'am." There was no escaping now.

"Do you want to tell me why?"

Was this a way out? What could I possibly say that wouldn't get me into more trouble?

My head spun as my mom stood there looking right through me with her blue eyes and talking to me with her *patient* voice. She was waiting.

"I didn't think you'd let me see it." I hated it when I sounded like I was three years old.

"And why was it so important that you see this movie?"

"Orlando was in it."

"Oh."

I didn't like the sound of that. Especially since she was holding my pillowcase. Why was she holding my pillowcase?

"Orlando Bloom?" she asked.

Was there another Orlando out there that I was madly in love with? Honestly.

"Yes."

My mom looked around my room. Her face seemed really sad for some reason. I didn't know why she was so sad when I was the one in trouble.

She handed me the pillowcase and opened my closet door.

"I want them all in here," she said.

"All what?"

She gave me that "don't get smart with me" look. I really wasn't trying to be smart; I was just trying to figure out what she wanted. It's not as if I'm a mind reader or something like that. So why is it every time *I* ask for a specific answer, *I* get accused of being a smart mouth?

"Your posters."

"My posters?" My mind still wasn't computing what she wanted. Or maybe I just didn't want to believe what she was asking me to do.

"Jenna."

Yep, I was in trouble. Her voice was *really* patient now.

"I want you to take everything that has a likeness of Orlando Bloom out of this room and stuff it in this pillowcase. Then I want you to bring the pillowcase downstairs and place it in the trash where your father and I can see it. Is that plain enough for you to understand?"

"Y-yes m-ma'am." I didn't mean for my voice to shake like that but it's hard to talk when you're trying not to cry.

I waited until my mom had left the room and then I stomped into my closet.

This wasn't fair. I wiped my nose with the corner of my towel. It was all Justin's fault. If he hadn't been so busy chasing girls he could have given me a ride home and then Will Addison wouldn't have even seen me, or recognized me. Now my nose was really running. Of course, if Mrs. Gilbert wasn't so nice and had to offer Will a ride then it wouldn't have happened either. That Will Addison was an idiot, standing in the rain and letting his battery go dead on his cell phone. And then opening his big mouth in the car and blabbing. It's not as if I looked eighteen. And come to think of it, what was *he* doing at an R-rated movie? He wasn't old enough to see them, either. Maybe I should call his mom and tell on him. That would fix him. Let him get in trouble and see how he likes it when someone blabs on him.

"I hate him!" I muttered as I pulled down the posters, being careful not to tear them. "I hate Justin, too!" I threw this in for good measure, just because I could hear him talking to Dad about football across the hall.

I don't know why I was being so careful with the posters. I guess I was hoping Mom would change her mind at the last minute. If they were going in the trash it wouldn't matter if they were torn or not.

And at that exact moment, I ripped one. A good one. One of Orlando with really dreamy eyes, the one that I always liked to look at right before I went to bed.

"It's not fair," I cried.

I had blamed everyone I could think of, but I knew it was my own fault and that's why I was really crying.

"I'm sorry, Orli," I said in my dramatic voice. I felt like I was breaking up with him. Not that I actually knew from experience what that felt like. It was more like I knew what it would feel like if it ever actually happened.

Orlando, we just can't be together now. I'm sorry to have to break your heart like this but my parents, they just don't understand. . . .

Mom probably would have let me go to the movie if I had asked her. It would have been the mature thing to do.

Yeah, right.

You never gave her the chance.

Sometimes having a conscience is a real pain.

All the lectures I had gotten recently about maturity and responsibility were coming back to haunt me. I really was acting like a big baby, blaming Will and Justin for something I had done, just because I got caught. It wasn't Will's fault that I did something wrong. He didn't even know me. How was he supposed to know that I wasn't allowed to see it? And Justin . . .

Sometimes it just made me feel better to be mad at Justin because Dad was always talking to him about football. I guess I was just jealous or something like that.

Being mature sure was a pain in the butt.

I realized I was still in a towel, so I put on a pair of sweats and a T-shirt and combed out my hair. No need to worry about how it looked. It's not as if I'd be going anywhere for a while.

I picked up the pillowcase. Might as well get it over with. I wondered if I'd actually be able to do it.

Everyone was sitting down for dinner when I arrived. Ellie came over and stuck her nose in my hand as I stood in the doorway of the kitchen, hoping that my Mom would think that I'd been punished enough.

My mom looked at the pillowcase and then at the trash compactor.

I knew there was no going back. It would go in and then the junk off our plates would go in after it.

I looked at Justin and could tell that he couldn't wait to scrape something disgusting onto Orlando. He'd probably laugh and make a big deal out of it, too.

I decided that I would be mad at him after all.

My hand was shaking as everyone watched me walk the million miles over to the compactor and step on the latch.

And drop it in.

I took a deep breath and waited. Nothing. Gee, I really thought I would faint or something like that. Nothing happened.

Then Justin had to open his big mouth. "What about that big cut-out that Gran got her?"

What a jerk. I wanted to smack him. No, I wanted to torture him. I wanted to cut his letter jacket and stick a knife in all his footballs and break all the little men off his trophies. I would pay him back, the traitor.

Have I mentioned how much I love my dad?

"I think we can leave that one alone," he said. "After all, it's from Gran." And that made it all right. Anything that Gran gave us was sacred and my mom wouldn't dare mess with it.

"You're dinner is getting cold," she said.

Take that, Justin! I sat down to eat but decided that I should pout some, just so they wouldn't think I had gotten off easy.

And I hadn't. My mom had gone right to the heart of me when she did that. How did she know?

As long as I had my posters I could dream about Orlando. And that was what I loved to do more than anything in the world. I mean wasn't it true that if you dreamed about something long enough it might just possibly happen?

Justin dreamed all the time about getting a college scholarship to play football and then turning pro. And from the sound of the dinner conversation it might just happen. It seemed like some colleges were interested in him and some scouts were coming to watch him play.

"I just hope that Addison kid doesn't screw things up for me and Ryan," Justin said.

Blah blah blah. I was so tired of hearing him complain about Will Addison.

"I don't know, Justin, I've been watching him at practice and he's got a great arm on him. And he can run the ball, too."

"Well, yeah," Justin had to admit. "But he's not in sync with the team. He doesn't know us."

"Maybe that's because you haven't given him a chance to know you," my mom said gently.

Justin kind of looked at her sideways with his fork halfway up to his mouth. How did my mom do it? She had just busted Justin and his friends big time without even changing her expression. It was almost as if she was a mind reader or something like that.

I knew that had been Justin's plan all along. Justin and Ryan knew Will Addison was good so they had decided to keep him as an outsider to make him look bad.

Guys are such idiots sometimes.

"He's different, Mom," Justin said, as if that explained everything.

"And what's so wrong with that?" my mom shot back.

This was getting good.

So why did the phone have to ring?

"I got it," Dad said. He knew my mom hated to have family time interrupted.

I hoped it was Jess. My mom hadn't said anything about not talking on the phone or anything like that.

My dad was suddenly very friendly to whoever it was on the phone. And then he handed the phone to me.

"Hello?" I said, not really sure what was going on, although my dad was smiling like that cat in *Alice in Wonderland.* "Oh, hi, Coach Miller."

"Jenna, we've decided to try you on varsity this year," he said. "I hope you're as excited as we are about the coming season."

"Uh, er, yeah," I said. I am such an idiot. "Thanks, er, I am excited." My family was looking at me. "Wow," I said.

"So we'll see you at practice in the morning. Nine A.M., so get a good night's sleep. The real work starts tomorrow."

"Er, yes sir, I'll be there. Thanks."

"Well?" my dad said as I hung up the phone.

"I made varsity."

"Cool!" Justin said.

"All right!" my dad said.

"Congratulations," said Mom.

"I never doubted it for a minute," my dad added.

"I wonder what happened with Jess," I said, suddenly terrified. What if she was on JV or worse, got cut? I'd be on varsity all by myself with all the upperclassmen.

"Why don't you call her and find out," my mom suggested.

Wow. Phone privileges. I *was* getting off easy. I picked up the phone and walked into our den. Ellie followed me. Sometimes I think animals can sense when you're worried about something.

"Hi, Mrs. Gilbert, this is Jenna." I used my polite voice. I figured she was mad at me for being a bad influence on Jess. "May I speak to Jessica, please?"

"Just a minute Jenna. I'll see if she's available."

Yeah, she was mad.

"Jenna, guess what," Jess said as soon as she picked up the phone.

"You made varsity?"

"Yes!" I moved the phone away from my ear and wondered how she could get her voice so high. "I know you did, too."

"How did you know?" I asked.

"Duh," Jess said. "You were awesome at tryouts. And Coach Miller told me."

"He did?"

"Well yeah, I asked him, silly. I told him we were best friends and it just wouldn't be the same if you weren't there. He said he thought we were a very good team and could tell that we'd played together for a while."

So why hadn't I thought to ask him? Now he probably thought that I was a moron. A tall stupid moron.

"So are you in trouble?" Jess asked me.

"Yeah. I had to take down all my Orlando stuff."

"Wow. That's harsh," Jess said. "I'm grounded for two weeks. And I had to have a heart-to-heart with my dad about honesty and stuff."

"I'm sorry, Jess," I said. "I shouldn't have made you do it."

"I should have made you not do it," she said.

My heart swelled. She really was my best friend in the world. And all I had done was get her into trouble.

"Jenn, I hope you don't mind, but I gave Will your screen name."

I—can't—breathe.

"He felt horrible about getting us into trouble and wants to apologize. I know he's online because his screen name is on my buddy list now and I can see him in his room at his computer."

"You can see into his room?" I checked to make sure that my family was still at the dinner table.

"Yeah, didn't I tell you that his room is right across the yard from mine?"

"So, what do you see?"

"Hang on." I could hear her messing with her blinds. "He's still there. Oh, and he doesn't have a shirt on."

"And?"

"He's buff."

"Well duh, he's on the football team," I said. I saw buff every day. I lived with Justin. So why did it feel like my face had turned red?

"He's dreamy buff," Jess said. "Oops, gotta go, the parental units are coming up the stairs. Buh-bye."

The phone clicked in my ear but I didn't turn it off. I just stood there, rubbing Ellie's head and thinking about what Jess had said.

Will Addison had my screen name. And he was sitting at his desk, all dreamy buff, waiting to apologize to me.

I can't breathe.

Chapter Seven

My room felt empty. Even though the posters had been in my closet, it still felt empty. Lonely. I flopped down on my bed and practiced my dramatic sigh in case someone was listening in the hallway. Even though I had made varsity I was still being punished. I had been hoping that my mom would relent and let me save my pillowcase, and I know they had even discussed it at the table while I was talking to Jess.

Justin had gotten up and been all *I'll do the dishes tonight* but my mom knew that he was just doing it so he could trash my pillowcase. At least he didn't get that pleasure, although he did look rather smug when he was excused from the table.

Or maybe he was just proud of me for making varsity. I had to laugh at that thought.

Anyway, then I volunteered to do the dishes but Dad said I needed to rest up for tomorrow and I probably should go to my room.

That was his way of saying stay out of your mom's way because she's still mad at you.

They've got that good cop, bad cop thing down pretty well.

So there I was, lying on my bed, missing my pillow-case and freaking out about being on varsity. I mean talk about pressure. Lots of people come to the varsity games. Lots. I know the entire football team does. The coaches all had this big thing about supporting each other's sports and our volleyball team was pretty good. They'd won the conference the past few years.

Our volleyball team. Geez, I was freaking. What if I sucked? Or worse, what if I never got to play and just sat on the bench.

That might not be so bad. At least on the beach I didn't have a chance to screw up in front of everyone.

My 'puter pinged me. I had an IM from someone.

What if it was Will? What was I supposed to say or type or whatever? I mean I've never actually talked to him, not really.

I looked at my screen.

IM's everywhere. Some were from Jess, some from the girls I had met at tryouts. Geez, news traveled fast—and then there were some from KHQB17. Kenton High Quarterback #17. It didn't take a genius to figure that one out.

Will Addison had IM'd me.

I pulled his box up.

KHQB17: sorry.
Legolass: *How does it feel to know you never have to be alone, Orlando?*

I never realized how stupid my away message was until now.

KHQB17: cool song.

Legolass: *How does it feel to know you never have to be alone, Orlando?*

KHQB17: maroon 5

Especially when I saw it over and over again. But you never know when some random person is going to IM you, so I'd figured I'd better be ready in case Orli ever did.

I am so stupid.

KHQB17: i'm full of regret . . .

Oh my gosh he was quoting Maroon 5 back to me. The lyrics from "Tangled." I love Maroon 5. They are like my all-time favorite band. Did Jess tell him?

Legolass: did you tell Will that I liked Maroon 5?

Potterchick: not yet

KHQB17: hey

I looked at my screen. I guess he saw my away message come down. So what was I supposed to do now?

Potterchick: did he IM you coz he's on rite now.

Legolass: YES!

Potterchick: and?????

KHQB17: sorry

KHQB17: r u n trubl?

Run trouble? What? Geez he can't even spell. Or was he making fun of my running? Wait, had he seen me run or something? We ran laps at tryouts. I must really look like a dork. I can't help it because my legs are long.

I—can't—

Wait a minute. Are you in trouble? That was what he meant.

Legolass: yes.

No wait. Then I'd have to explain about the posters. I mean my punishment would sound kind of stupid to someone else. Big deal, she had to take her posters down. She gets a new pillowcase. Most people got grounded, like Jess. Hey, what was Jess doing online if she was grounded? Usually that was part of the punishment. I'd have to ask her about that. Later, that is.

Legolass: i mean no
Legolass: NO
Legolass: not really
Potterchick: WELL?
Legolass: i thought you were grounded.
Potterchick: i am. they forgot about this.
Legolass: k

KHQB17: i don't mind spending every day
KHQB17: in the pouring rain

More Maroon 5.

KHQB17: :)
Legolass: don't bother.
Legolass: you'll get sick

Did that sound stupid? I felt sick to my stomach. It *was* stupid. Geez, I probably sounded like his mother or worse, my mother.

KHQB17: lol
KHQB17: i'd deserve it
KHQB17: i'm really sorry
Legolass: don't worry about it
Legolass: so what were u doing in an r movie?
KHQB17: my mom took me and my friend
KHQB17: she has this thing for brad pitt.
Legolass: ewwww

Now that was dumb. I just dissed his mom.

KHQB17: i know. he's like ten years younger than her.
Legolass: sounds like my mom. she has this thing for russell crowe.

There, I dissed my mom, too.

KHQB17: moms are weird.
KHQB17: but mine is really cool sometimes
Legolass: yeah
Legolass: mine too
Legolass: sometimes.

Not today, though. Although it really could have been much worse. I looked around my room. After all, Orli had pretty much been banished already. Except for the pillowcase. And my cut-out was still standing in the corner so I could see it when I fell asleep.

I had an elf protecting me. Awesome.

KHQB17: so you like LOTR?
   Huh? Oh, *Lord of the Rings*.
Legolass: yeah, how'd you know that?

This guy must be a stalker. I mean he was quoting Maroon 5 and everything. Now he knew my favorite movie. I swear if Jess has been blabbing I will kill her. .

KHQB17: duh
KHQB17: your screen name
KHQB17: LegoLASS???

Good thing he couldn't see me. My face had to be really red.

Legolass: yeah. i think legolas is awesome
Legolass: elves are awesome
KHQB17: me 2
KHQB17: two towers is my favorite.
KHQB17: helms deep
KHQB17: cool fight stuff

Typical guy. They just like the fight scenes. But it was really awesome when Orli rode the shield down the stairs and fired his bow. And I had to admit Viggo was awesome even though I wish he'd take a shower or at least wash his hair.

KHQB17: i liked it when the elf guy rode his shield like a surf board and shot everyone.

Oh my gosh!

Legolass: me 2
Legolass: how bout when he killed the olifant in the last one?
KHQB17: yeah that was awesome
KHQB17: lol
Legolass: what
KHQB17: olifant
Legolass: that's what sam called it.
KHQB17: do you have it all memorized

Geez.

Legolass: so what if I do?
KHQB17: sorry

Potterchick: talk to me
Legolass: can't
Potterchick: you're talking to him
Legolass: yes
Potterchick: and????
Legolass: nothing
Potterchick: I can see him

Legolass: and?
Potterchick: nothing
Legolass: puleeeze
Potterchick: he's drinking milk.
Potterchick: he is soooo hot!
Potterchick: he's wearing shorts and a tank top

Legolass: someone is spying on you
KHQB17: ?
Legolass: look out your window

I waited.

Potterchick: you told him
Legolass: haha
Potterchick: he waved at me
Potterchick: he has a great smile
Legolass: really?

Yeah, he did. I remembered it from the van. All white and dimply and his eyes matched it. Nice smile.

Legolass: awesome.
KHQB17: so you mad at me?
Legolass: ?
Legolass: no
KHQB17: congratulations on making vball
Legolass: yeah
Legolass: thanks
KHQB17: gotta go. got to get up early for practice
Legolass: me too

KHQB17: maybe I'll see you there.
Legolass: maybe
KHQB17: g'night

Please don't say sweet dreams, please don't say sweet dreams, please don't say sweet dreams . . .

KHQB17: Dream away everyday . . .

Maroon 5 again. His away message went up. I wondered what it said. Should I find out? What should I say?

Legolass: see you tom
KHQB17: *two-a-days ouch!*

Geez, he sounded just like Justin.

Chapter Eight

I couldn't sleep. I was too wired. My bed felt weird, or actually just my pillow. My mom had thrown a pillow-case into my room while I was brushing my teeth.

She must still be mad. I wrestled my pillow into it and plumped it up the best I could. I got out my iPod and put on Maroon 5.

Wasn't it funny that Will liked them, too? Of course, nearly everyone I knew liked them, but how many people could quote the words like that.

He probably had the CD case sitting next to his 'puter. I wonder if Jess can see *that* from her window.

I listened to "This Love" and before I knew it I was freaking about volleyball practice.

Our first game was in a week. What if I screwed up? What if Coach Miller decided he had made a mistake? What if everyone hated me? And worse, what if they made fun of me?

Why couldn't I just concentrate on Orlando instead of worrying about all this other stuff? I didn't want to have dreams about playing volleyball naked or something weird like that. I needed my pillowcase. I mean I had a ritual and everything! No wonder I couldn't get to sleep.

I decided to go downstairs and have a bowl of cereal. I really hadn't eaten much at dinner, what with being punished and then the phone call from the coach. Maybe if my stomach wasn't growling I'd be able to sleep. I'd better get used to going to sleep early again. School started next week.

Ellie greeted me from her bed in the hallway. She always had trouble figuring out which room she wanted to sleep in, so my dad had solved the problem by putting her cushion at the end of the hall and that way she could keep an eye on all of us.

Ellie followed me downstairs, of course. Anyone going to the kitchen was fair game in her mind. As long as I was down there I might as well check the trash compactor to see how bad the damage was.

Empty. Did they actually think I would dig my stuff out of the trash?

I fixed myself a bowl of cereal while Ellie watched me with her big hopeful eyes. She knew she was going to get the milk when I was done.

"What are you doing up so late?" Justin asked as he came into the kitchen.

"What does it look like I'm doing?" You'd think he was king of the world or something the way he acted. I flipped the pages of my mom's decorating magazine that was lying on the table as I ate.

Justin ignored me and went to the fridge.

"Gross!" I yelled as he drank straight out of the milk jug.

"Shut up," he said and gave me his cocky smile. He was so conceited. Just because every girl at school was falling at his feet all the time.

"Cut it out," I said back.

He looked at my cereal bowl and must have decided that it looked good because he fixed himself one, too, and sat down across from me at the table.

"Do you always have to make so much noise when you eat cereal?" I asked. Ever since we were kids and sat in front of the TV on Saturday mornings he would always slurp his cereal and then make a funny noise when he swallowed it. It drove me nuts.

"Mom, make him stop," he said in a very bad imitation of my voice. He gave me his cocky grin again.

I just rolled my eyes at him. Did he actually think that stuff was going to work on me?

"So it's pretty cool that you made varsity," Justin said. He looked at me and I noticed that his eyes were more green tonight than usual. Just like Gran had said.

"Thanks."

"Carrying on the tradition and all that." He acted like he was actually proud of me or something.

"Yeah."

"The games are always on Thursdays, so we watch game films and then go watch the team," he explained. "That is if you're playing at home."

"Yeah," I said. It's not like I haven't been paying attention for the past couple of years.

Gross. He was drinking out of the bowl.

"So there will be a lot of people there." He wiped his mouth on his T-shirt.

"So?"

"So don't screw up." He messed up my hair on top and dropped his bowl in the sink on his way out.

"Can't you at least put it in the dishwasher?" I said, knowing that he would ignore me.

I put my bowl on the floor so Ellie could drink the leftovers and then made sure the kitchen was straight. Justin always left crumbs lying around and never rolled the wrap down around the cereal so it wouldn't get stale. And he'd find a way to make it look like it was my fault. He was good at that. Especially during football season.

No need to give my mom another excuse to be mad at me. Ellie followed me back up and pushed the door of my mom and dad's room open and went in.

I remembered that I had left the light on downstairs so I ran back down to turn it out.

Then, remembering that I should be considerate and mature and stuff like that, I walked very quietly back up.

I could hear my mom and dad laughing in their room. The door was still open, courtesy of Ellie.

"I still think we should send her to drama school," my dad was saying.

Were they talking about me? Were they serious? Drama school? I could really be an actress and make movies with Orli?

"Did you see her face when she carried that pillow-case down? It was all I could do to keep from laughing. You would have thought we'd ask her to kill Ellie," my mom said.

They were making fun of me. Geez, my own parents thought I was a joke.

"Don't you think you were a bit harsh?" my dad said.

Have I told you how cool my dad is? I crept closer to the door and prayed that the floor wouldn't creak beneath me.

"No. She needs to do something besides sit in that closet and moon over Orlando Bloom."

"She's got the volleyball," my dad pointed out.

Yeah Dad!

"And she's got her friends and she's got us but she still spends a tremendous amount of time mooning over some movie star." I could see my mom's face in my mind, explaining why this was all so important. "I just want to make sure she doesn't miss out on her real life because she's always in her imaginary one."

"I seem to remember some pictures that you had on your wall back in the day," my dad said.

"I did not."

"Yes you did. Who was it?"

"You're thinking about your other girlfriend," my mom said. A bit defensively I might add. I knew about defensive. Or so my mom claimed.

I heard the rustling of the sheets.

"Oh yeah, I remember. It was Johnny Depp. From *21 Jump Street*."

"Shhh," my mom said.

"No wonder you couldn't wait to take her to *Pirates of the Caribbean*," my dad laughed.

"You're imagining things."

"I've got your imagination right here," my dad said.

GROSS!

Ew.

Yuck.

I am going to throw up right this minute.

I ran as quietly as I could to my room and shut the door firmly behind me.

I could have gone my entire life and not heard that.

Gross.

Chapter Nine

"Justin, you're taking Jenna and Jessica to practice this morning," my mom said. "And bringing them home at lunch."

"Mom!" Justin whined. He slammed the refrigerator shut. "Why do I have to do it?" You would have thought she had asked him to take me shopping for underwear or something the way he was carrying on. And they said I was dramatic . . .

"Because I'm meeting a client," my mom said with her patient voice. "And it would be a waste of gas for both of us to drive to the same place at the same time, now wouldn't it?"

My mom laid a twenty on the counter. "This is for breakfast and lunch," she said. "For *both* of you."

Justin snatched the twenty and stuffed it in his pocket. He grabbed a banana and took off towards the driveway. "You're going to have to help me get the top down," he yelled as he went out the door.

"Thanks, Mom," I said.

"Make sure you let Ellie out when you get home," my mom said.

"Okay, I'll do it."

My mom stopped getting her stuff together and looked at me.

"We're really proud of you for making varsity," she said. Then she hugged me. "Go kick some bootie," she said.

Bootie? Gross.

"I'll try," I said.

"Jenna!" Justin yelled. Then he beeped his wimpy horn just to make sure I heard him.

"Coming," I yelled back. Geez, he is so impatient. You would think the world spun around his life.

It really was a nice day. A great day for riding with the top down. I didn't mind. My hair was in a ponytail anyway. Having the top down was fun. The rain from last night had made it less muggy. No wonder he was looking forward to practice. It wasn't nearly as hot as it was yesterday. I hoped the gym would be cool, too.

We hit the drive-through for fast food and then headed to Jessica's.

Justin started laughing when we got close to her street.

"What's so funny?" I yelled over the wind and the speakers.

"There goes our second string quarterback," he said. "Hey dufus, maybe you should quit playing ball and get a job so you can drive somewhere." He yelled that part but it got lost in the music and wind from the Jeep.

I turned around and saw Will Addison jogging down the street in his practice clothes.

"He's only a sophomore," I said. "He doesn't have his license yet."

"Well aren't you a font of information," Justin said. "What else do you know about him?'

"Nothing," I said.

"I heard he's the one that got you in trouble with Mom," Justin said. I didn't like the look on his face.

"He didn't know that I wasn't supposed to be in there."

"He shouldn't be butting his nose in where it doesn't belong," Justin said.

"Quit being such a jerk."

We had pulled into Jess's driveway and I climbed into the back of the Jeep. I was sick of listening to Justin complain about Will Addison.

Jess, of course, was thrilled to get to ride up front with Justin. I watched as she played with her hair and acted all mature and stuff. Justin was flirting back, as usual. Doesn't he ever get tired of putting on a show? At least I didn't have to talk to either one of them since the wind and music were so loud.

Then I saw Justin point. Will was running down the side of the street. He had his shirt off and it was tucked into the back of his workout shorts. He looked pretty good, like the running wasn't wearing him out too much. But then again it was two-a-days. He'd be worn out by tonight.

"There's your neighbor," he said. "Think I should run him over?"

"No," Jessica swatted his arm in mock horror.

Oh please. I'm going to throw up.

I leaned forward between the two of them.

"Give him a ride," I said.

If Mom had heard the words coming out of Justin's mouth at that exact moment she would have had a meltdown.

"Give him a ride or I'll tell," I said. It's not easy to be threatening when you're screaming in someone's ear.

"Tell what?"

"Well for one thing, what you just said, and another, remember what Mom said at dinner last night about giving him a chance?"

"Ryan will kill me," Justin said.

"Ohhh," I said in a scary voice. "Since when are you afraid of Ryan?'

Ha ha. That got him. He wasn't happy but he swung the Jeep over and slammed on the brakes coming up right behind Will. He turned around and his face had this look on it, like he was kind of ticked.

I stood up in the back and waved.

"Hey, Will, need a ride?" I yelled.

Justin popped the clutch and I had to grab for the roll bar. I smacked the top of his head with my other hand.

Will smiled at me. One of those wide smiles with lots of teeth and his eyes getting crinkly and his dimples going real deep.

Justin let his foot off the clutch again. The Jeep jumped right at Will.

"Sorry," he yelled. "Are you coming or what?"

"Stop it, Justin," I said between my clenched teeth.

Will grabbed the roll bar and jumped into the back-seat right as I was sitting down. Justin chose that moment to step on the gas, and I wasn't ready.

Do I even have to tell you where I fell? I mean what are the chances. He has to think I'm some sort of pervert.

I could hear Jessica squeal and then she laughed.

Justin was driving like a maniac. I swear I don't know how he got his license. Will pushed me up. I could hear him laughing, too.

"We've got to quit meeting like this," he said.

That had to be the corniest line I had ever heard, not that I've heard that many. I knew my face was bright red and my eyes were wet. I wasn't really crying, not really. I think they got wet because I was burning hot. And to think that I had thought the first time was humiliating. At least he didn't know who I was then.

But it was also a sweet line. I mean he could have called me a pervert or something worse—was there anything worse?

"Jenna," Justin yelled. I could see his eyes in the rearview mirror. They were stormy gray this time. "What in the heck are you doing?"

He didn't say heck by the way.

"Quit driving like a maniac!" I yelled back.

"Is he your brother?" Will asked.

"Unfortunately," I said.

Will looked the other way for a minute. I think he was trying to stop laughing.

"So why were you running?" I asked. I mean talk about your awkward silences.

"My mom's sister is having a baby. My mom went to stay with her at the hospital last night. Then my dad had an emergency at work. I just told him I'd run to practice and not to worry about it. It's only two miles from our house."

"Where does your dad work?"

"He owns a tool repair business in Kenton," Will said.

"How far is that?"

"About forty-five minutes," he said.

"So you just moved here to play football?"

"Yeah." He looked away again. I think he was embarrassed about it or something.

"Cool," I said. "I think we're supposed to be pretty good."

"That's what my dad said."

Justin was watching us through the mirror. I knew he couldn't hear us. He should probably keep his eyes on the road instead of the backseat. I made a face at him.

"So do you have family there?"

"Yeah," he said. "Both sets of grandparents and my mom's sister and her family. But she's in the hospital here. There's not one in Kenton. Just a clinic, I think. We always came here for our doctor's appointments and to shop at the mall and stuff."

"Must be kind of boring, living in a small town like that."

"Not really," he said.

He must be lonely, I realized. I mean really lonely. He had lived in the same town his entire life and all his family was there and all his friends and then right when it's time to go to high school and life gets good and fun, his dad packs him up and moves him to another town where he doesn't know anybody at all. And all because his dad wants him to be a big football star? I mean was it really worth it? Sometimes I think the parents get into the sports thing more than the kids do. I mean don't get me wrong, I really like volleyball and everything, but it's not like my life is going to be over if I don't get to play it again. I have other . . . interests.

But guys are different. They really get into it. I mean Will must really like football a lot. He could have told his dad that he wanted to stay put. Maybe he really wanted to move. Maybe playing football is the most important thing in the world to him and he wants to be part of a team that really does well and then get a scholarship to State and maybe get drafted into the NFL. Maybe he came here hoping that it would be really cool.

And then my brother goes and acts like a big jerk to him.

Geez, I was starting to sound like a guidance counselor.

"Do you have any brothers or sisters?" I asked. Jess hadn't seen any but that didn't mean they hadn't left any of them back in Kenton.

"I have a sister," he said.

"Is she nice?" I made a face towards Justin.

Will laughed. "She is now. Since I'm not a pest anymore. She's seven years older than me. She's getting married this December."

"Are you going to be in the wedding?'

"Yeah. Get to wear a tux and everything."

"Awesome." I bet he looked good in a tux. He looked pretty good in shorts, too.

Jessica kept turning around. She was trying to figure out what we were talking about.

We pulled into the parking lot and Justin drove at least ninety miles an hour toward the gym, not even really slowing down for the speed bumps. I felt like I had whiplash by the time he screeched to a stop in one of the parking spots.

I saw Ryan do a double take when we pulled up. He was going to be ticked for sure.

Justin just jumped out of the Jeep and took off for the gym, leaving the rest of us to catch up. The idiot slammed the door so I either had to lean forward over the seat to open it, climb over the side, or get out on Jessica and Will's side.

Will held the seat up for me.

"Thanks for the ride," he said. Did I mention that he was taller than me? At least a couple of inches. I actually had to look up to see his face.

"No problem," I replied. Did that sound cool? We walked to the gym with him and said some see-ya-laters as he turned to go toward the locker rooms.

"Omigosh," Jess said when he was safely out of earshot. "He's so hot! Tell me what you talked about. What did he say last night? What did you find out?"

"There's nothing to say," I said and went on into the gym for practice.

"What?" Jess said. I think she was shocked. I didn't

say anything else as we lined up in front of the coach. It was time to practice.

What could I say? We had talked and it was nice. That's all.

Besides, I wanted to think about it for a while.

Chapter Ten

We got out of practice at 11:30. Volleyball was going to be pretty cool, Jess and I decided. Coach Miller had us working as a team and was telling us how he was going to rotate us in and out so that I was never in the back row and Jess would never be in the front.

Then he placed me with a couple of the taller seniors and we worked on blocks and kills. Blocks are all about the timing. You've got to figure out where the ball is coming over and get there at just the right time, then you jump with a teammate with your arms up, being careful not to go into the net. I think I did okay at blocks.

Kills was another issue. I guess I just wasn't strong enough or something like that. You've got to make sure you hit the ball on the way down or else it will go flying off into the deep backcourt or else up in the air. And if you hit it too low it will go into the net. I did get some over but they were soft or something.

Coach Miller said he wanted me to get mean. I didn't know what he was talking about but I nodded and pretended like I did. I was just worried about looking stupid more than anything.

Jess had worked on bumps and serves. She was already good at setting. She had a light touch and could set the ball pretty much wherever she wanted. Coach said later he'd have her do some setting for the hitters. We decided we'd work on it by ourselves that afternoon.

Jess and I walked down to the football field to wait for Justin. We knew it would be at least a half hour until he was done and it was as good an excuse as any to look at cute guys.

Not that I was really looking.

I had decided that I should feel sorry for myself since I had been punished. I mean I had spent a lot of time and a lot of money on mags and stuff just to get the most perfect pictures of Orlando. And they were all gone, just thrown in the trash like they were nothing. Even the one that Jess had gotten me for my birthday. Gone.

And you don't even want to know how I agonized over winning that pillowcase on eBay. Then I had to beg Mom to let me use her credit card to pay for it. I even had to give her the cash I'd earned babysitting up front. She hadn't been happy about it, either, but when I explained that I had already won it and I couldn't not pay for it she had given it over with a warning to check with her first next time.

Guess there wouldn't be a next time now.

And besides that, if I acted like I was in a funk I wouldn't have to answer all of Jess's questions about Will Addison.

I mean what did she think had happened anyway? All we did was talk. Really, how serious can you get in the backseat of a Jeep that's going ninety with the top down and the stereo thumping?

And last night all he had done was apologize for getting me in trouble.

How did Justin know he had been the one to tell on me anyway?

He had to have found out from Jess or my mom and dad. I really didn't think Mrs. Gilbert was a possibility.

"Did you talk to Justin last night?" I asked Jess.

"He IM'd me," she said. She got all glowy like it was something special. "He was teasing me about getting caught at the movies."

"Did you tell him how your mom found out?"

"Yeah." Jess looked at me. "Why?"

"Because Justin was mad at Will because he was butting into our business." We had reached the stadium and were walking across the bleachers to the shady spot in front of the press box. Some of the girls from the team were already there, hanging out just so they could flirt. Geez.

"What's he going to do?" Jess asked.

"Make life worse for Will," I said.

"He already hates him," Jess said. "What more could he do?"

I just kind of shrugged. I didn't like it. Justin had been majorly ticked this morning, especially after I made him give Will a ride.

We sat down to watch practice.

They guys were all wearing their pads and helmets.

I noticed a couple of players had on red jerseys while everyone else was in white with those net things on over top of them to say if they were offense or defense. The two in red had to be the quarterbacks. Which meant one was Ryan and one was Will.

Will was taller than Ryan, although he was skinnier. They were pretty easy to pick out.

They were taking turns at doing plays or something. One would take the snap and stuff would happen, then the other one would get on the line and do pretty much the same thing.

I always wondered why a guy would want to be a quarterback. I mean he had to put his hands up under another guy's crotch. Gross. Maybe it would be worse to be the center and have the guy put his hands there.

I didn't want to think about that. Especially if the center guy had been eating at Taco Bell.

There was a lot of running around going on, then one of the coaches would blow their whistle and either yell at them or tell them they did a good job. I couldn't figure out which team was supposed to be doing better, the offense or the defense. You wanted both to be good so who was supposed to be winning out there on the field?

They lined up again. Ryan did this thing called shotgun where he stands back and the center hikes the ball at him. Justin came flying around the end, past the guys who were supposed to be protecting Ryan and pushed him back. I watched as they laughed. I guess Ryan knew that Justin could have put him on the ground if he wanted to.

The coach blew his whistle and they lined up again.

This time Will did the shotgun thing. Justin came flying again.

But Will moved out of his way. Justin ran past him and as he did Will stuck out his hand and shoved him away so that Justin kind of tripped for a few steps, then Will threw the ball down the field to one of the guys who was supposed to catch it. The receiver. I've been watching football almost my entire life and I still can't remember what all the words are.

The whistle blew and some of the guys gave Will some high fives. I noticed that he didn't say anything, just went back to his place off to the side to watch as Ryan came in to do a play. But then the coach waved at him and told him to come back and line up. I felt sorry for Ryan. He looked kind of lost as he went over to where he was supposed to stand.

"Uh oh," I said. "Justin is mad." I could tell just by looking at him. He didn't look like he was having fun anymore. His hands were clenched up into fists as he lined up.

"Justin's going to kill that guy," one of the older girls that was hanging around said. I noticed that they all were kind of looking at me.

They did the snap thing again. Will kind of stepped back a couple of steps. He was looking around for someone to throw the ball to.

And then one of the guys who was supposed to be protecting him just stepped out of the way. Justin ran through the opening and nailed Will in the gut with his helmet. Will went flying to the ground. He landed on his stomach and didn't move for a while. The coaches were all blowing their whistles and I saw one of the coaches grab Justin's face bar on his helmet and pull it down so he could yell at him. Another one grabbed the guy who had stepped out of the way and yelled at him, too. The rest of them gathered around Will.

Will rolled over on his back and I think everyone was amazed to see that he still had the football.

Then Will sat up and somebody offered him a hand but he just ignored them and stood up on his own.

I knew his side had to be killing him and the trainer was trying to get a look at it, but Will just shook his head and flipped the football to Ryan as he walked over to the place on the side where he was supposed to wait.

"That was some hit," I said to Jess.

"He's awesome," she said. I knew she was talking about Justin.

But I had been talking about Will.

Chapter Eleven

Luckily Will's mother showed up so I didn't have to worry about giving him a ride home. We watched as he got into the car with her. She even asked him if he wanted to drive since he had his permit and he said no.

He looked stiff. I think Justin hurt him and he just wasn't letting on.

I waved as they drove by but he ignored me. He had his head laid back and his eyes closed.

"Do you think he's hurt?" Jess asked.

"Wouldn't you be?" I snapped. She ignored me. She knew I was angry.

"Yeah, or dead," she said.

We hung around, waiting, as usual, for Justin. He was supposed to get us lunch before he took us home and I was starving.

He finally showed up, laughing and carrying on with Ryan.

"What took so long?" I asked.

"The coach wanted to talk to me," he said.

"Are you in trouble?"

"For what?"

"What you did to Will?"

"What's with all this Will stuff? Suddenly you're all Will this and Will that and give Will a ride and feel sorry for Will because nobody likes him." He started the Jeep and took off, ninety miles an hour again.

"Nobody has had a chance to like him," I muttered from the back. Then I realized he hadn't answered my question.

"Are you in trouble?"

"For what?"

"Tackling Will like that."

"Hey, he wanted to play four-A ball, he's going to have to take four-A hits. He's not in that bush league anymore. He's up with the big dogs."

"But he's on your team."

"I'm not in trouble, Jenna. Just shut up about it."

I saw his eyes in the rearview mirror and he was giving me this look. I knew what it meant. Don't tell Mom and Dad what happened and I won't make your life miserable.

Brothers are such a pain.

And then he started doing the flexing thing while he was shifting for Jess. Have you ever noticed how guys will push up their sleeves and rub their arms just so you can look at their muscles?

Gross.

We pulled into Wendy's and Ryan followed us. He was still high-fiving Justin in the parking lot like Justin was his hero or something.

Will Addison must be pretty good. I mean I had

seen him get away from Justin in practice. He probably could have again if the guy who was supposed to have been guarding him hadn't moved.

Justin probably told him to move so he could hit Will. And Ryan was scared that Will was better than him.

Guys are just stupid sometimes. I mean they were all talking about winning a state championship and stuff like that, so didn't they want the best chance to do that? If Will was a better quarterback than Ryan then shouldn't he be playing so they'd have a better chance to win?

But then again, Will was an outsider. The rest of these guys had been playing together since they were like six years old and started Pop Warner football. That was back when my dad and Ryan's dad coached together and taught them fundamentals and stuff.

So who should be playing?

I'm glad it wasn't up to me to decide. Coaches really had a tough job. I mean I bet Coach Miller had caught all kinds of junk from some of the parents because their daughters had got cut from varsity and me and Jess made it.

"I think we should practice a lot on our own," I said to Jess. "I mean we don't want to screw up or make the team lose or anything like that." I took a sip of my Diet Coke. "Since we're freshmen," I added.

"Yeah," Jess said.

"You'll be fine," Ryan said. "Coach Miller wouldn't have put you there if he didn't think you could do it."

Geez, a compliment from Ryan. He must be feeling pretty good right now. I even smiled at him.

"I bet you broke a couple of ribs with that hit," Ryan said to Justin. "I was hoping that he wouldn't get up."

And just when I thought he was being a nice guy.

"Probably," Justin said and grinned real big. "I was surprised when he did."

I threw a fry at him.

"What?" he said.

"You guys are just jerks," I said. Suddenly I wasn't hungry anymore. I grabbed my drink. "I'm going to wait in the Jeep."

"Jenna," Jessica whined.

Great. Now she was probably mad at me. She was all happy and stuff because we were sitting in Wendy's with Justin and Ryan and everyone that drove by could see us.

I didn't care. I was tired of my brother being a jerk.

"Talk about major PMS," Justin said. "I think it's turned into a permanent thing."

I was too angry to answer. I wanted to kick him or hit him. How could he be such a jerk? How could we even be from the same family? I heard Justin and Ryan laughing at me as I left Wendy's.

I climbed into the back of the Jeep and lay down with my legs hanging out over the side.

Geez!

I sucked on my straw and looked at the clouds that were drifting overhead. I tried to find images in the clouds but they were the long stringy kind instead of the fluffy ones that were fun to look at. Gran and I used to study the clouds when I was little. We would lie on the pier by the lake in our bathing suits and see what kinds of animals we could spot. Sometimes, on warm nights, we'd go out in our pajamas and take our blankets and look for shooting stars and stuff.

Of course, Justin was always included. I mean I didn't expect Gran to love one of us more than the other. And sometimes it had really been nice. Peaceful. Innocent, my mom would say. That was all before Justin got into high school and was so worried about being cool.

How could he have turned into such a jerk? I mean it wasn't like Will was going to kill Ryan or something. Why did they have to be so mean to him?

What if Will really did have broken ribs? He *had* looked a little sick when his mom picked him up.

I heard someone walking across the parking lot. Probably Jess . . .

"Hey," she said. She opened the door and got in the passenger seat. "Are you okay?"

"Yeah," I said. "I just get so tired of them being such jerks."

"They're just being guys, you know," she said.

What did she know about it?

"What's Icy Hot?" she asked.

"Why?"

"I heard them talking when I was dumping my tray. They said something about Icy Hot and started laughing."

"It's something Justin puts on when his muscles hurt," I said. I wondered what that was all about.

"They're coming," Jess said.

I knew they were. I could hear them laughing.

"Later," I heard Ryan say. "Bye Jenna!" he yelled as he got into his car.

"Whatever . . ." I said. "Jerk."

Justin drove to Jess's at ninety miles an hour again. I knew he was doing it on purpose because he kept looking at me in the rearview mirror. I had to keep a good hold on the roll bar to keep from getting bounced around, even with my seat belt on. I swear if Mom knew how fast he drove she would take the Jeep away.

Of course, he'd never do anything that stupid when she was around.

I looked to see if there was a car in Will's driveway when we got to Jess's. There was. So maybe he didn't have broken ribs. If he did, they'd be at the hospital getting X-rays or something like that.

Or maybe he didn't tell his mom about the hit.

"Are you getting up front?" Justin asked after Jess got out.

"Whatever," I said. It would look stupid for me to be riding in the back with the passenger seat empty. I climbed over the console and plopped down in the seat.

"I guess your boyfriend's mommy can bring him to practice tonight," Justin said as we backed out of the driveway.

"He's not my boyfriend," I said and rolled my eyes. As if!

So why was I looking at the upstairs window, which I knew belonged to Will's bedroom?

Justin was such a jerk!

Chapter Twelve

Jess called after I got out of the shower and said her mom would bring her over later to practice. Justin had already left. Ryan had a pool and he said he was going to go hang out there and rest. More likely they were plotting more attacks on Will.

Ellie made herself comfortable in my bean bag, her new favorite place, while I went online to catch up with my e-mails. I noticed that Will's name was on my buddy list now, a result of our chat the night before. His away message was up and I couldn't help but be curious so I highlighted it to see what it said.

KHQB17: *two-a-days ouch!*

So why should it be anything different? What did I think it was going to say? I'm dying because Justin Wheeler tackled me?

Oh yeah, my away message needed to be changed. I went to the edit and looked at what it said.

How does it feel to know you never have to be alone, Orlando?

So what should I put? Something cool. Something high schoolish. I mean I *was* going to be a freshman in just a few days.

This was harder than I thought . . .

I got up from my 'puter and flopped on my bed. Ellie padded over and stood there with her tongue hanging out, waiting for me to rub her head.

"So what should I say, Ellie?" I asked as I rubbed her ears.

She closed her eyes and enjoyed the rub.

I heard a door close downstairs.

"Let's go see Mom," I said and she followed me out.

"How was practice?" Mom asked. She was putting away some groceries and handed me a bag of stuff to put in the fridge.

"Fine," I said. "Jess is coming over so we can work on some skills."

"I'm glad you both made it," Mom said.

"Yeah, me too." There were grapes in the bag she handed me so I washed them off in the sink and put them in a bowl. I noticed that Mom was smiling as she put the food away and realized that I had done something without her asking me to.

Isn't it funny that sometimes you don't even realize that you're growing up, that you just . . . grow? Or maybe it's maturity. It's kind of scary when you think about it.

"Mom?" I asked.

"Hmmm?"

"We're not ever going to move, are we?"

I sat down on one of the bar stools and plucked a grape.

"Probably not. You're dad's company is here and there would be no reason for him to leave it."

"Yeah," I said. I rolled the grape between my fingers. I wasn't really hungry. Ellie watched my hand as if I was holding a steak or something. I guess she was hoping I'd drop it.

"Don't feed her grapes," my mom said. "They're not good for her."

"It must be hard to move to a new town and have to start all over again," I said.

"It is, sometimes," my mom said. "But then again, sometimes it's an adventure. You're starting something new and exciting. And there's all kinds of possibilities."

"Kind of like starting high school?"

"Yes, or going off to college, or getting married," Mom said. "A new beginning if you want it."

"What if you don't?" I asked. "What if your parents made you move because of their job or a divorce or they didn't like the school you were going to before?" I rolled the grape around on the counter like it was a ball. "What about that?"

"Sometimes parents make decisions that they think are best for their children, even if the children don't like them at first. Parents have the ability to see the long-term effects. Children mostly look at the short term."

"Oh," I said.

My mom looked at me. "Is Jessica's family moving?" she asked.

"No," I said. Wow. That was a scary thought. "Not that I know of."

"So what's got you so worried?"

"I just was thinking about that new guy at school that's on the football team," I said.

"Will Addison?" she asked.

"Yeah, Will Addison. I was just thinking that it really wasn't fair that his dad made him move just because he wants him to play football in a big high school so he could get noticed."

"Maybe Will Addison wanted to play football in a big high school, too."

"Maybe," I said. I thought about the conversation we had when riding in the Jeep. He never came out and said that he was happy about moving here. Just that his dad had thought it was a good idea.

And his parents had made a lot of sacrifices to move here. I mean his dad was driving almost an hour each way to work and all their family was back in Kenton and stuff. I bet his sister wasn't happy about it, either. I mean she had lived there her entire life and now she had to get used to a new place. But then again she was getting married so maybe she didn't care.

A sudden image of Will Addison in a tux entered my mind. His hair was flipped up over his ears and he was holding a box with a corsage in it. Weird. It usually was Orlando in a tux and he was always holding this giant engagement ring. Where did that picture of Will come from?

I needed to quit thinking about this guy so much. Geez. Maybe I should quit talking about him, too. I didn't want people to think that I liked him or something.

So what if I did? Now that was really weird. I felt almost like I was betraying Orlando or something.

"What's wrong, sweetie?" My mom asked.

"Nothing, why?"

"You just got this really strange look on your face," she said. She was staring at me with those blue eyes of hers, like she could see right through me.

I stuck the grape in my mouth. It was all hot and squishy. I kind of choked on it and my eyes watered. Mom handed me a glass of water.

"Are you sure you're okay?" she asked.

"I'm fine," I said. The doorbell rang. Jess had arrived, and just in time. I figured I better get out of the kitchen before my mom started reading my mind or something, so I herded Jess straight out to the backyard.

"What's your problem?" Jess asked when I threw her the volleyball that was sitting on our deck.

"Nothing." I could see my mom watching us through the window. "She's just still kind of mad at me," I lied.

Then I felt bad. Jess just kind of looked at me while she spun the ball around on her fingertips. I knew I was acting weird but I couldn't really explain it. Plus I had just made my mom look like the Wicked Witch of the West when she had really been kind of cool.

"Let's practice," I said.

We worked on sets and spikes and bumps and blocks the best we could without a net. Mostly we just chased Ellie around because she went after the ball every time we let it get away. It got kind of slobbery and I eventually had to go wash it off with the hose.

"I guess I'm going to have to build you a court out here," my dad said. "We could fill it with sand and make it beach volleyball."

"Cool!" Jess said.

I looked around our yard and then at my dad. Yeah, he was serious. Suddenly I saw the potential. Jess and I could practice and then maybe after a while we could have a party or something with the team. My imagination took over and I saw the lights on the deck and some of my friends hanging out and sitting in the hot tub and stuff and of course Justin was there and Ryan . . .

And Will Addison.

I was really starting to have a problem with this guy. It was almost as if he was haunting me.

Or maybe it was just my imagination. It was almost as if he was becoming an . . . obsession.

I should probably concentrate on something else.

"So, what do you think?" my dad asked.

Yeah, volleyball. Concentrate on volleyball. No, wait, think about Orlando. Yeah that's it. Think about Orlando.

Since when did I have to make myself think about Orlando?

I probably looked like a big dork just standing there in the backyard with my eyes all glazed over.

"Earth calling Jenna!" Jess said. She faked throwing the volleyball at my face.

"Awesome," I said. I gave my dad my best smile. "I think that would be awesome."

"Your mom called," Dad said to Jess. "I told her I'd take you home on my way over to watch practice."

"Thanks, Mr. Wheeler," Jess said. She was all glowy again. Looking at my dad and thinking about Russell Crowe I'll just bet.

"Can I go with you?" I asked my dad.

"I'm going straight to practice after I drop Jess off," my dad said again. Like I didn't know that.

"I know. I want to watch, too," I said.

"You want to go watch football practice?" I asked Jess.

"I can't, I've got to babysit," she said. She gave me a funny look. I realized that she was probably mad at me now because I suddenly had this cool idea to go watch practice and she was stuck babysitting.

I gave her an *I don't know what came over me* look while my dad fussed over Ellie.

Yeah, she was mad.

"Maybe you could get out of it?" I suggested.

"Grounded," she replied. "That would just make it worse."

No doubt, she was mad.

"Probably shouldn't even try," my dad added. He put his arm around her shoulder. "It's all Jenna's fault," he said. "We raised her to corrupt everyone around her." Wow. He could really turn on the charm when he wanted to. So now I knew where Justin got it from.

"Dad!" I said. It was kind of embarrassing to watch

my Dad flirt with my friend. Or maybe I was just jealous or something.

"It's okay, Mr. Wheeler. I was easily led astray," Jess said. She didn't seem so mad anymore. I mean she wasn't really going to miss anything. All it would be was sitting around on the bleachers listening to a bunch of dads talk about how awesome their sons were. Still, she made me promise to call her cell if anything happened.

It was neat hanging out with my dad. Everyone said hey to us as we found a place on the bleachers and some even congratulated me for making volleyball. My dad had a big cheesy grin on his face, so I knew he was proud of me. It felt pretty cool.

"Dad?" I asked. "What's Icy Hot for?"

"You put it on your muscles when you're sore," Dad said. "Why? Are you sore from practice?"

"No, I was just wondering. I heard Justin and Ryan talking about it today like it was a secret or something."

Technically Jess had been the one who heard them, but after what had happened at practice this morning I just wanted to make sure they weren't up to something, although I couldn't even imagine what it could be.

"You did?" Dad said. "Hmmm . . ." He got this strange look on his face, and then he started grinning as he looked out on the practice field.

"Excuse me." A man came up to my dad and offered his hand. "I'm Bill Addison. Just wanted to say thanks for giving my son a ride to practice this morning." It was easy to see where Will got his height from. His hair, too.

"David Wheeler," my dad said, shaking hands. "And my daughter, Jenna." Dad looked at me. "I guess my son Justin gave him a ride."

"Yeah," I said to my dad. "We saw Will running when we picked up Jess."

"Well, we really appreciate it," Mr. Addison said. "Will hasn't had a chance to make any friends on the team yet, but he has mentioned you and our neighbor."

My dad gave me a look but it had a smile attached to it. "It must be hard on your son, moving into a new school and a new team. I'm sure Justin would be happy to give him a ride when he needs it."

Yeah, Dad. Right.

"Will's going for his license in a few weeks, so it shouldn't be too much of a problem."

"That's always a big load off when they start driving and you don't have to haul them around," my dad said. "But then again it's a whole different set of worries."

"That's for sure," Mr. Addison said. "We've got a daughter who's getting married in a few months. I know about worries. You just got to do what you think is best for them."

My dad laughed. "Even if they don't always agree with you."

Geez Dad, getting kind of personal real quick here.

"It wasn't an easy decision to make, moving and all," Mr. Addison said. "But we felt it was the best thing for Will." Just like my mom had said. Parents doing what they think is best for their children.

My dad nodded in agreement. I looked around to

see if Ryan's dad was here. He'd probably have a fit if he saw my dad talking to the enemy.

"So I hear you're the president of the Booster Club," Mr. Addison said.

Wow. Mr. Addison must have done his homework. The Booster Club was my dad's passion. Dad was telling him about meetings and stuff and Mr. Addison was already volunteering to work the concession stand and give money or anything else the club needed. I bet they missed Will's parents back at Kenton as much as they missed Will.

"He's looks a bit stiff out there tonight," Mr. Addison said when they quit talking long enough to look at practice.

The team had finished up with their stretching and warm-ups and had split up into groups. I instantly found Will. It wasn't hard, since there were only two guys out there in the red jerseys. It didn't take a genius to know that he was sore.

"He must have taken a hit this morning," my dad said. He was looking at me again.

"If he did, he didn't mention it," Mr. Addison said.

I kept my eyes on the field. No way was I getting into the middle of this. Justin would make my life miserable and I didn't need him angry with me just when I was starting high school.

I wondered why Will didn't say anything to his parents. It wasn't as if it was a big secret or anything. I mean everyone that had been around this morning knew he had taken the hit from Justin.

Maybe I should tell my dad. Then again, maybe I

shouldn't. I mean it was guy stuff and they had this code or something weird like that in sports. I guess Will just thought that everyone would think he was a big weenie if he said something.

But he had to be sore. He probably shouldn't even be practicing. But there he was, doing that line of scrimmage thing. At least that's what my dad called it.

Justin was lined up on the end where he usually was. He was really fired up.

"Your son looks like he gives it a hundred percent every time," Mr. Addison said.

"A hundred and ten," my dad said. I wondered if he ever talked about me that way.

The ball was snapped and Will took a few steps back while the linemen did their protection thing.

I heard Justin yell as he pushed against one of the linemen.

"There he goes," my dad said.

Justin jumped through an opening. Will must have seen him out of the corner of his eye because he ducked just as Justin reached for him. At the same instant that Justin missed Will, Will came up with his shoulder. Justin landed flat on his back and Will threw the ball downfield towards one of the receiver guys. It was kind of a wimpy throw, probably because he was sore.

My dad kind of whistled or something. I don't think I'd ever seen Justin get tossed like that before.

Will reached his hand out to Justin to help him up.

I tried not to throw up. I just knew Justin was going to smack his hand away or something.

But he didn't.

I think everyone around was holding their breath as Justin let Will pull him up.

"He looks pretty good," my dad said when Justin had run back to his side.

"Yours does, too," Mr. Addison said.

"I'd say we've got a pretty good shot at States this year," my dad added.

"That's why we're here."

Geez, they sounded just like Justin and Ryan talking.

"Might want to tell your son to keep a close eye on his, er, equipment, in the locker room," my dad said. He kind of winked at Mr. Addison but he was looking at me when he said it. "I heard a rumor that there might be some Icy Hot showing up. Kind of an initiation thing I guess."

"A little present in his jockstrap?" Mr. Addison said. "Wouldn't be the first time Will's had that happen, or the last."

I'm pretty sure my face turned bright red as I realized what they were talking about. I mean I knew what a jockstrap was for and where it went.

Oh my gosh!

Icy Hot in the jock.

Icy Hot in Will's jock. That would have to hurt. Wouldn't it?

Oh my gosh . . .

I.

Can't.

Breathe . . .

Chapter Thirteen

I made it all the way to lunch on the first day of school without doing something stupid. I felt like celebrating. I had managed to find all my classes. I could open my locker without any trouble. And my skirt wasn't too short, which was something I had freaked over all week. I had nightmares about being made to wear some ratty old gym clothes because the principal found my clothing to be inappropriate or something like that.

Jess and I had some classes together, which was really cool, and better yet, we had lunch at the same time. I didn't have to worry about being alone in the cafeteria!

Justin and most of his friends had lunch the period before us. He smacked me on the arm when he passed me and Ryan made this weird smoochy sound with his mouth.

Gross.

Why couldn't they just act like normal people?

Oh yeah, because they're guys.

Duh.

Lunch at the cafeteria was the usual high calorie, high carb fare. Chicken nuggets and French fries. Pizza and chips. There was salad, but it looked really old, which was strange since it was the first day of school. Had they been saving it since last year? I settled for some fruit and a bag of cheetos. I knew I'd be starving after volleyball practice.

Jess and I found a table and we tried to look like we were really cool and sophomores instead of just freshman that were scared out of our minds. It's all about the attitude. That is if you can carry it off without falling flat on your face. I thought I was pretty lucky that I hadn't dropped my tray.

"Hey, there's Will," Jess said.

I turned around and saw Will coming our way with a blond guy that was a few inches shorter than him. The blond guy had the most perfect hair I had ever seen.

"Hey!" Will said as they walked up to our table. "This is Scott. He's the punter."

"Hey," Scott said.

"What's a punter?" Jess asked.

Have you ever seen anyone snort juice out of their nose? I couldn't help it. It was like a really stupid question, at least it was for me since I spent half my life going to Justin's games. But then I had to bury my face in my napkin and I know my face was bright red. Why did I act like an idiot every time I was around Will Addison?

"I kick the football," Scott said.

"Oh," Jess said. She looked down at her tray.

"I'll explain it to you while we eat," Scott said and sat down right next to Jess. She scooted over against the wall and looked at me with a big cheesy grin on her face.

Will was still standing there holding his tray so I moved over and he sat down next to me.

"How are you?" I asked.

Scott was already telling Jess all about kicking field goals and stuff.

Will looked at me kind of strange. "Fine. Why?"

"Oh, I thought you might be sore or something. You know, from last week?"

Why hadn't I learned to just keep my mouth shut? I mean Will was probably embarrassed about Justin hitting him so hard and didn't want anyone to know. Now he probably hated my guts since I had brought it up.

Will just shrugged. "It's part of football," he said.

"Yeah, we've learned to live with it," Scott said. "Besides, he got Mr. Superstar Defensive End back."

"Um, Scott?" Will said.

"Ambushed him in the locker room," Scott continued. "Wheeler and his buddy were plotting to put Icy Hot in Will's jock, but Will got him first."

"What did you do?" I asked Will.

"Not a thing," Will mumbled. He must have kicked Scott under the table because Scott jumped and gave Will a look.

"What did he do?" I asked Scott.

"He put itching powder in Wheeler's Gold Bond."

"Oh," I said. "OH!" I said again when I realized what Justin used Gold Bond for.

Jessica covered her mouth as she laughed.

"By the way, genius," Will said to Scott. "This is Jenna Wheeler, Justin's sister."

Scott made a horrible face.

"I guess I'm a dead man," he said.

I grinned at him. "Nope. I think you're a genius," I said. "Both of you. Wish I had thought of it."

"Is your brother as big a pain at home as he is here?" Scott asked.

Okay . . . now what was I supposed to say? I could say Justin was a pain, which he was, and make Scott feel cool for dissing Justin. Or I could say no, he wasn't and then Scott would feel bad for dissing my brother. My mother would probably frown upon me dissing Justin. We were family. We were supposed to stick together.

Then there was the question of what Justin would do when he found out I had dissed him. For that matter, what would Justin do when he found out that I had lunch with the enemy? He was going to be mad and I was pretty much screwed no matter what I said.

"He's her brother, dufus. He's supposed to be a pain. At least that's what I tell my sister," Will said. He looked at me and I couldn't help but notice again how brown his eyes were. Just like Orlando's. Brown and soft and dreamy . . .

"I wouldn't know," Scott said. "Only child."

"Oh, you are so lucky," Jess said. "I have a little brother and he is a big pain."

Jess was flirting big time with Scott and he was flirting right back.

"So where do you get itching powder?" I asked Will. "It might come in handy sometime."

"It's gag stuff," Will said. "Someone pulled it on me last year at Kenton."

"Do you get picked on a lot?" I asked. Oh no. Another stupid question. What guy is going to admit that he gets picked on without sounding like he's a big whiny geek?

"Kind of," he said. "I'm always the youngest on the team or the new guy. Kind of makes you a target."

"I guess it does."

"I was watching out this time," he said. "I knew it was just a matter of time before something happened."

Then he did the coolest thing. He leaned over and whispered in my ear.

"Your brother just about killed me," he said. "He's really awesome."

I felt really strange. Kind of proud of Justin but then again kind of goose bumpy because Will was telling me a secret. He didn't want anyone else to know how much Justin had hurt him. Yet he could tell me, Justin's sister, that he had. I mean how did he know that I wouldn't run home and tell Justin what he had said?

And just then I realized that I wouldn't tell Justin what he had said. I wouldn't tell anyone. It was a secret. Something just between me and Will.

Me and Will.

Geez. Justin was going to kill me.

"What are you two talking about?" Jess asked.

"Nothing," I said.

Will just grinned and went back to eating his lunch.

I managed to make it through the rest of the day without a disaster, which to me is a great accomplishment. Practice was cool. We were going to have our first game at home on Thursday and Coach Miller was really getting us pumped up. My mom picked me up from school and took me by the drugstore to get some notebooks and other school supplies.

When I got home I got on my 'puter and did some research. School stuff and movie stuff. Orlando was filming a crusader movie and I was dying to see some stills from it. Too bad I had to wait until next summer for it to come out. I thought it was cool that he did all these historical movies. I mean I was actually learning stuff from watching his films.

At least that was the argument I was going to use on mom when his next movie came out. Or maybe I wouldn't have to. Maybe his next movie would have a PG-13 rating and I wouldn't have to worry about it.

The smell of dinner cooking drifted up the stairs. I thought about helping Mom set the table or make a salad or whatever. I heard Justin's Jeep roar into the driveway. He had two speeds with that thing. As fast as possible and screeching on the brakes. The door slammed and I heard him pounding up the stairs.

"What's wrong with you?" he yelled.

I leaned back in my chair to see who he was talking to. He stood in my doorway, still all sweaty and dirty from practice. His hair was sticking up all over and his face was bright red.

"What's up?" I asked.

"You had lunch with Will Addison."

Yeah. To say he was furious was putting it mildly.

"So?"

"So what's wrong with you?" He was yelling. Really yelling. Ellie walked over to him and wagged her stubby tail. Justin ignored her. "You can't eat lunch with him. You can't even talk to him."

"Why not?"

"Because I hate his guts, that's why."

"Just because you hate him doesn't mean I have to," I said. I turned my back on him and looked at my computer screen. "Just because you're a jerk doesn't mean I'm going to be one, too." I closed down the screen I was looking at. "You don't even have a good reason to hate him. You don't even know him."

"Oh and you do? What are you, the welcoming committee for student transfers?" He walked into my room.

I rolled my eyes. Clever, Justin, really clever.

"I know that he's a nice guy and he wants to fit in."

"You like him."

"Get out of my room, you're stinking it up." I wasn't about to get into an argument with Justin over whether or not I liked Will Addison.

And what if I did?

"Stay away from him, Jenna. I mean it."

"Get out," I said. I refused to look at him but I knew he was behind me. I could hear the beads my mom had hung up swaying.

Then I heard this weird thunking sound. I turned around and saw my Legolas standee kind of crumpled up in the corner.

"You punched my Legolas!" I yelled.

Justin had a smirk on his face. I wanted to smack him. I did smack him on the arm. Not that he'd feel it or anything.

"That's what I'm going to do to your boyfriend, too," he said.

"What is going on up here?" my mom said.

"Justin hit my Legolas!" I wailed. I was crying. I could not believe that he could be that mean. How could anyone be such a jerk?

"Justin, go take a shower," my mom said. "And we're talking when you get done."

"She's a traitor, Mom." Justin said. Then he rubbed his arm. Right where I had hit him.

Hah! He did feel it. I heard him stomp off while I picked up my standee. It was bent and creased, right at the neck.

"He ruined it!" I cried.

"Jenna. It's just a piece of cardboard," my mom said.

I was so mad I was shaking.

"You just don't understand!" I said in my dramatic voice. It worked, too, because I was all shaky and stuff.

My mom looked at me with her blue eyes. I could see that she didn't understand. She didn't understand at all.

Orlando. Please come rescue me!

I fell on my bed and grabbed my pillow. Except my pillowcase was gone, dumped in the compactor and covered with trash and sent off to the dump where it would lie buried for thousands of years.

I knew my mom was looking at me. I didn't want to look at her. She should make Justin pay. She should make him buy me a new one. I mean it had been a gift from Gran and everything. It was the only Orlando thing I had left. It wasn't just a piece of cardboard. It was . . . special.

My mom shut my door on her way out.

Chapter Fourteen

I—can't—breathe.

I looked across the court at the stands in our gym as I stood on the sideline waiting for the ref to allow me to sub into the very first game of the season. It was really hot and the air was thick and kind of smelly from everyone being inside. There was a big fan blowing by the door, but it was still hot. My shirt stuck to my back and the hair in my pony tail felt damp on the ends.

Gross.

I could feel my lungs going in and out but I really couldn't breathe. I felt like I was going to fall flat on my face at any moment.

My mom and dad were there and my grandparents and Jessica's parents of course and her brother and all the other girls' parents and parents from the opposing team and then there was the football team. They were all fanning themselves with our team roster sheets and drinking bottled water like crazy. I would have been happy just to swallow. The lump in my throat felt like a volleyball.

How many people were here? Hundreds? Thousands? Millions?

Just the thought of all those people gathered in the gym watching me play volleyball made me want to hyperventilate, at the very least.

That is if I could manage to breathe.

Just breathe.

The ref wrote my number down on his card so he could make sure that I didn't get out of rotation and the girl I was subbing for gave me a high five as she walked off the court and I walked on and took my place in front of the net.

"Come on Jenna!' my dad yelled.

"Go Seventeen!" Someone else yelled.

Seventeen was my number. Talk about coincidence. That was Will's number. He had been seventeen at Kenton and he had gotten seventeen here, too. And then when they were handing out uniforms to our team I ended up with number seventeen. It was just too weird for words. Justin even commented on it. Said it was a sorry number and it was too bad I had to wear it.

My mom had smacked him in the back of the head when he said it. She knew I was nervous enough without Justin jinxing my number or something weird like that.

I had managed to get through the first few days of school without having any disasters. My skirts weren't too short, I didn't drop my tray in the cafeteria and I managed to find all my classes and remember my locker combination. My classes were okay, although I didn't really like my algebra teacher.

All in all, high school was turning out to be okay. Except for lunch, that is. I mean Jess was still there and everything, but Will and Scott didn't eat with us after that first day. We saw them and they said hey and stuff but they went to their own table and sat with some other guys. I didn't know if Justin had said something to Will or not. I didn't know if I should even ask. If I said anything and Justin had said something it would just mean that Will was scared of Justin and no guy wanted to admit that he was scared. It was like it was against their religion or guy code or something. Jess was freaking. She thought Scott was really hot. She even said they'd been talking online and stuff.

Anyway. High school was okay.

Until now. The first volleyball game. The first home volleyball game. I just knew I was going to do something stupid. I mean, how long could I go without looking like an idiot? It was inevitable. My luck had to change soon. It was a big mistake for me to be on varsity. Big mistake.

"Woo-hoo Jenna!" my mom yelled.

Geez.

Don't think about it.

Don't listen to the crowd.

Just play.

And breathe . . .

It was our team's serve. One of the senior girls was

serving. She ran up to the back line and did an overhand serve that dropped right towards their back row.

I moved up to the net as their back row bumped it towards the setter.

The setter pushed the ball up off her fingertips towards one of their hitters. The two other girls on our front line came running over to me.

I just knew their hitter was going to aim for me because I was just a dumb freshman and would screw up.

All three of us jumped up as the ball came flying towards my end of the net. We stretched our arms up and blocked it!

At least the other girls blocked it. I never touched it, but I did jump up when they did so it looked like teamwork and the crowd cheered as the other team dove for the ball and missed.

Hey, we got a point.

And I didn't do anything stupid.

Yet.

Wow! This was cool. Everyone on our side of the net was clapping and giving me high fives and saying "Way to go, Jenn!"

Awesome.

I kind of looked at the crowd as we lined up to serve again and noticed my mom and dad were all smiling and stuff.

This was cool!

We served again and it was out-of-bounds, so we lost the serve. I took a deep breath. The other team was getting ready to serve and was rotating and subbing, so our team got in a huddle. The team captain was talking about how awesome we were but I just kind of looked at the crowd while we were huddled up.

The football team was sitting together at the end of the bleachers. They were all wearing shorts and their practice jerseys. I could see Justin and Ryan and all their cool friends sitting together and I knew they were checking out the girls while they were bent over in the huddle.

Will was there with Scott and the team but it looked like they had come in last, so they had to sit at the edge of the group. At least some of the players were talking to them; or at least it looked like they were. I noticed Will was nodding and smiling and when we broke from the huddle he clapped his hands and said "let's go" or something like that.

I went back up to the net.

The other team served and I got all tensed and ready. The ball went over the net towards our back row. I turned to get ready. Our back row bumped it towards the setter.

"Get ready Jenna!" someone yelled.

The setter popped the ball up—right towards me.

I jumped up and swung my arm. I gave it everything I had as I brought my arm around. I hit the ball—right into the net.

I watched the ball like it was in slow motion as it hit the net and stretched it back like a slingshot.

It hit the bottom of the net and came flying back out, but I had stopped watching it as soon as it hit the net. If I had been watching it I would have seen it come back out. I would have seen the ball come flying back at my face.

I did see it right before it hit me in the eye. And knocked me flat on my back.

I—Can't—Breathe.

Is my nose broken? Geez. It has to be. I can't feel it. Oh my gosh.

I felt for blood.

Gross.

Everyone that had been on the court was in a circle around me, looking down at me. They were talking to me but I couldn't hear them because the blood was pounding in my ears.

Could the floor open up and swallow me? *Please? Now?*

I managed to sit up. Coach Miller was there and he had his hand under my arm. He was probably going to throw me off the team.

"Can you stand up?" he said.

Noooooo! Everyone will see me!

I stood up and everyone cheered and clapped.

I don't think I've ever been more embarrassed in my life. And I've done some embarrassing stuff, believe me.

Coach Miller led me to our bench and someone handed me a towel. I sat down and stuck the towel under my nose. Someone else handed me a bag of ice for my eye.

I looked at the bleachers and I could see everyone was looking at me and pointing and my mom was getting up to come over and check on me.

Please . . . . . . noooooooooooo.

And then the strangest thing happened.

Will got up and ran down the front of the bleachers to the other end.

He stuck his arms up in the air.

"Do a wave!" he yelled.

Oh my gosh. A wave at a volleyball game. Was he crazy or something? Everyone would make fun of him.

He ran down the length of the bleachers. I could see my mom coming down and she was looking at me and not paying attention to where she was going.

Will wasn't paying attention to where he was going, either, because he was yelling and had his arms up in the air. But nobody was paying attention to him. They were still looking at me and pointing and stuff.

My mom stepped off the bleachers.

Will crashed into her.

Will and my mom grabbed each other's arms and she laughed and he laughed and then some people in the stands laughed, too. At least they didn't fall on top of each other. I think I would have died then.

Then my mom pointed to where the football team was sitting.

"Do the wave!" she yelled.

Will ran back to where he had started and this time the crowd paid attention to him. He ran down the length of the gym yelling at everyone to do the wave. My mom got everyone up where she was standing and then the coaches from the football team stood up so the team had to do it.

And then Will ran the length of the gym again.

And again.

And my mom went back into the stands and I realized that no one was looking at me anymore. They were doing the wave and cheering and watching the game.

That's when I realized that Jess had gone in and she was doing pretty well at serving.

"Come on Jess!" I yelled.

"Woo-hoo Jessica!" someone yelled.

It was Will.

But this time he was sitting kind of in the middle of a bunch of guys and they were whooping it up.

But he smiled at me.

At least I think he did.

It's kind of hard to see with one eye swollen shut.

Chapter Fifteen

My mom made me go for X-rays after the game. We won, by the way. Three straight games. Nothing was broken, but I had a shiner.

And according to the doctor and my dad there was no reason for me not to go to school the next day. I had to show how tough I was.

Justin thought it was all pretty funny.

Jerk.

I went to my room with another bag of ice for my eye and dug around in my drawers for a pair of sunglasses. I found a pair but they were small and didn't really cover up much since most of the bruising was on the side of my eye. The good news was that I found my stash of Starburst that had been missing since my mom redecorated my room.

Maybe it was time to think about wearing bangs. I chewed on a Starburst and folded my hair back in the front so that it looked like bangs. There was no way makeup was going to cover up the big bruise on my face.

Geez, I was such a klutz. How many volleyball players clobbered themselves with a missed spike?

And the entire football team saw it.

Why was I on varsity? Why couldn't I be on JV? No one came to those games. Maybe the coach would let me move down.

Or maybe he'd throw me off the team since I was such a klutz.

If only I didn't have to go to school tomorrow. I'd have all weekend for the bruising to fade. Maybe everyone would forget about it over the weekend.

Yeah, like that was going to happen.

I lay on my bed and considered all the things that could happen before the next day that would get me out of going to school.

Bomb threat?

It could happen but not likely. Not unless I wanted to call one in and with my luck I would get caught and sent to prison for the rest of my life.

Flood?

It was the end of August. Hot and cloudless. Miserable, as a matter of fact.

Maybe I should think on a smaller scale.

Fever?

Not from a black eye.

Oh . . . dizzy spells. That was reasonable. I mean I had taken a severe blow to the head.

Okay, so when I got up in the morning, I'd have a

dizzy spell. I practiced throwing my hand up over my eyes and acting dizzy, like I was going to pass out or something.

And just because I was thinking about passing out I might as well pass out in someone's arms.

And the only arms I wanted to pass out in were Orlando's.

I looked at my standee. The head was kind of leaning forward from Justin's punch. If Justin had punched the real Orlando he probably would have punched him back. Knocked him flat on his butt.

I had a great fantasy going. Orlando decks Justin because he's being a jerk and then he realizes that I'm not feeling well and I go weak in the knees and he has to catch me and he apologizes because he thinks I'm upset about him hitting my brother but I'm not, I just have this tragic illness and he has to carry me to my bed and stay by my side night and day and nurse me back to health.

All the tabloids talk about my death watch and then I recover, miraculously of course, and it's all because of Orlando's love and devotion.

Maybe we could have a reality show about the entire thing, kind of like Nick and Jessica's newlywed show on MTV.

Cool.

Someone pinged me on my IM so I rolled off the bed and tossed the bag of ice into my bathroom sink. It was all melted now anyway and it's not like it was helping. I was already black and blue around the eye.

KHQB17: how ru?

I really needed to change my away message. Unfortunately I hadn't had time to come up with anything cool.

Legolass: ok
KHQB17: nothing broken?

Geez. Had I looked that stupid? Did everyone think I belonged in a body cast? I needed to be cool about this, or else I'd never be able to show my face at school again. And considering it was the first week of my freshman year . . .

Legolass: just my image . . .
KHQB17: lol

Okay, was he laughing at me today or laughing at me now? Or maybe he was laughing with me.

Legolass: just how stupid did i look?
Legolass: can I show my face at school tomorrow or should I think about transferring?
KHQB17: i thought you looked great!

Wow. I wasn't expecting that. Was he just making that up? I mean I looked like an idiot, didn't I?

KHQB17: you were great on the block and the spike looked awesome except. . . .

Legolass: except for the hitting the net part?
KHQB17: yeah. and the hitting your face part.
Legolass: i admit it. i'm a klutz.
KHQB17: hey we all are at one time or another.
KHQB17: except for maybe your brother.
KHQB17: lol
Legolass: you mean mr. perfect?
Legolass: he's been laughing about it all day.
KHQB17: put some itching powder in his gold bond.

Oh yeah! I had forgotten about that. Will had turned the tables on Justin. I bet he wasn't so high and mighty dancing around in the locker room with his boxers on fire.

Legolass: lol. good idea. got any that I can borrow?
KHQB17: hang on

Maybe I should remind Justin about that the next time he is smirking at me.
Will pinged me again and it was a link to some novelty gag site. So that's where he got his ammunition.

Legolass: cool.
KHQB17: yeah. you never know when you might need some of this stuff.
Legolass: got a credit card I can borrow?
KHQB17: my sister lets me use hers

Legolass: yeah, I can see that happening with Justin.

And then I realized that I had forgotten about my black eye. Just talking to Will had made me forget about how humiliated I had been. Just like at the game when he had jumped up and done the wave so everyone would quit looking at me and start looking at him instead.

It took a lot of courage for him to do that. I mean everyone could have just ignored him or worse pointed at him and laughed, just like they'd been pointing and laughing at me. Okay, so I didn't really see anyone point and laugh, and I know that my parents wouldn't do that, but I bet some people thought about it. Plus, I couldn't see that well with one eye swollen shut.

Anyway, it took a lot of courage for Will to stand up in front of the crowd—and they'd actually done the wave. Of course, my mom had been out there, too, and she's pretty bossy and gets her way a lot.

Wow.

Will was really cool.

Legolass: thanks for what you did today.
KHQB17: what did i do?
Legolass: the wave. it was cool.
KHQB17: just showing my school spirit.
KHQB17: go panthers!
KHQB17: you can pay me back at a football game.
Legolass: what?
Legolass: do the wave?

KHQB17: sure.
KHQB17: why not?

Oh my gosh. I had a vision of me running up and down the sidelines at a game trying to get everyone to do the wave. There was a very good reason why I had never gone out for cheerleading.

Legolass: no way
KHQB17: why not?

Was he insane?

Legolass: because I would probably fall flat on my face.
KHQB17: lol
KHQB17: i'd help you up.
Legolass: from the field?
KHQB17: from the bench
Legolass: you're going to play.
Legolass: i watched you practice.
Legolass: you're awesome
KHQB17: you watched me get killed by your brother.
KHQB17: i'm still sore.
Legolass: my dad said you were awesome too.
KHQB17: really?
Legolass: yes really.
KHQB17: cool
KHQB17: so are you coming to school tomorrow?
Legolass: yeah.

Wait a minute. I was supposed to go to school tomorrow. But I wasn't going. I was going to get dizzy or something.

KHQB17: want to meet for lunch?

I—can't—breathe.
Was this like a date or something? What should I do? What should I say? I mean Justin had already pitched a fit and Will had basically ignored me since the first day of school, which was really only a few days ago.

Geez, I was freaking out and it was probably nothing. I mean he was just asking me to eat lunch together in the cafeteria.

Legolass: sure.
KHQB17: cool.
KHQB17: see you tomorrow.
Legolass: see ya

His away message went up.
I really should change mine.

Chapter Sixteen

Okay. My list of nicknames for the day was really getting long. Spaulding was getting a lot of attention. Everyone kept saying they could read it on my forehead.

Yeah, right. I just happened to be trapped in a school full of comedians.

I just laughed. It was either that or cry. My dad had driven me to school that morning. He told me I was going to get baptized by fire and to keep my chin up. By lunchtime I had finally figured out what he meant by that.

Coach Miller had called me to his classroom during my first period. He wanted to make sure I was okay and tell me that he expected me to be back in the game next week.

I was pretty sure he just wanted me around because my dad was president of the Booster Club and would make sure the team got whatever they needed.

I'd probably be sitting the bench for the rest of the year, which was fine with me. I mean how much trouble can you get into just sitting on a bench?

Knowing me, probably a lot.

That made me remember what Will had said last night about sitting the bench during the season. It was kind of depressing. I mean he moved and everything just so he could play football at a good school and get noticed by college scouts and all he was going to do was sit the bench? Maybe he should have stayed in Kenton and played.

It was all so confusing. How do parents know when they're making the right decisions for the good of their kids? It's not like they can see into the future. I know there's all that stuff about life experiences and things like that, but how do they really know? What if it didn't work out and Will sat the bench for the next three years and it was all for nothing?

Wow. I was getting depressed just thinking about it.

I had IM'd Jess last night and told her that Will was meeting me for lunch. So then she wanted to know if that meant Scott was meeting us, too. Like Will was meeting both of us instead of just me.

But why should I think he was just having lunch with me? I mean it's not like he could call up the cafeteria and reserve a table for two. And Scott did have lunch at the same time as the rest of us.

I was totally confused about the entire situation by the time I walked into the cafeteria. And I hadn't seen Will in the hall between classes like I usually did, either. I didn't know what to expect.

Guys are such a pain. At least I was spared the privilege of seeing Justin and all his poser girlfriends before lunch. My English teacher had been going on about something and we were late getting out. Figured that it would happen today of all days.

"There's Scott," Jess said as we walked into the cafeteria.

Sure enough, there he was sitting by himself at a table. He waved at us.

"Hey," we both said.

"Where's Will?" I asked.

"Getting his license," Scott said. "His year was up today. He was supposed to be back by now."

"The DMV must have been crowded," Jess said.

"It's always crowded." Scott said. Then he looked at me with a big grin on his face. "Nice shiner."

Don't say it. Don't say it. Don't say it.

"Spaulding," he said.

Geez. Had they announced it over the intercom or something?

"Shut up," I said. I was getting a little tired of it. And I figured I could sass Scott if I wanted to. At least with him I wouldn't get a bad rep. I think . . .

Will was getting his license. I remembered his dad had said that he would get it soon and then he wouldn't have to worry about getting to school and practice and stuff.

I think the driving laws they have now are stupid. You have to wait an entire year after getting your permit to get your license, even if you're already sixteen. And the driving classes at school are hard to get into because everyone wants to take them. So it's hard to get your license on your sixteenth birthday unless you take private lessons or something. I mean, do they really think that a few more weeks of driving are going to make that big a difference?

"When did Will turn sixteen?" I asked.

"The end of July," Scott said. "He's really supposed to be a junior, but his dad redshirted him when he was in kindergarten because his birthday was so late." Scott and Will must be getting pretty tight if Scott knew all these personal details about him.

Oh yeah, redshirting. That's when you sit the bench for a year so you can get bigger and stronger for sports. I guess it applied to kindergarten, too. Or maybe he was just kidding. I guess my parents could have redshirted me since my birthday is in August. But then again, everyone knows that girls mature faster than boys. And I was always the tallest one in my class.

I was probably going to be redshirted off the volleyball team for the rest of the year.

Ha!

Jess and I got in line to get our food.

"I wonder if Will's parents are buying him a car," Jess said. "Maybe I could ride to school with him."

"Your parents won't let you ride to school with him," I said. For some reason I didn't like the thought of Jess riding around with Will. "You know how much they freak out about that kind of stuff."

"It's not any different than me riding with Justin," she said.

"Yes, it is. When you ride with Justin, I'm in the Jeep, too," I explained.

"Having a dad that's a minister is a curse some-times," Jess said as she paid for her food.

"Maybe they won't care since Will's your next-door-neighbor and they know his parents," I said.

"Yeah," Jess sighed. "Maybe."

We took our trays and went back to the table.

Will was there.

Sitting at the table.

He looked unhappy. Kind of saggy through the shoulders.

"You don't think he flunked it, do you?" Jess hissed at me as we walked up to the table.

"Don't be ridiculous," I hissed back. "Nobody flunks their driving test."

"Hey!" I said.

Will looked up at me.

"Ouch," he said. I waited for him to move over so I could put my tray down but he didn't budge.

"Yeah, it's been fun."

"Just call her Spaulding," Scott said. Jess had al-ready slid in next to him.

Will just sat there. He didn't say anything else. He didn't even call me Spaulding.

I felt pretty stupid just standing there holding my tray. Especially since I had a black eye and everything.

"Are you going to eat?" I asked. I had to say some-thing. People were beginning to stare.

"Nah," he said. "I'm not hungry."

Then he got up and walked out of the cafeteria.

As if! I'm pretty sure my jaw dropped about a mile.

"Sit down," Jess said. She was looking around to see if anyone was watching.

I slammed my tray down on the table and sat down with a dramatic huff. At least I hoped it was dramatic and not whiney or anything like that.

"What's up with him?" I asked.

"What do you think is up with him?" Scott said. For some reason he acted all ticked off at me.

"He flunked his driving test?" I asked. I think the word to describe my reaction is incredulous.

"Yeah."

"How did he flunk?" This had to be some kind of joke.

"He went through a yellow light. He said he didn't know if he should stop or go so he went and the guy flunked him."

"Oh." I looked through the window of the cafeteria. I could barely see the top of Will's head as he walked through the crowded hall. He was kind of slouched down instead of walking tall like he usually did.

"Bummer," Jess said.

"Yeah," Scott said. "We had plans for tonight. This was our last free Friday night before football starts."

The first football game was next Friday. I knew Justin and Ryan had big plans for tonight, too. I'd probably just stay home and watch TV with Mom and Dad.

"So when can he take it again?" Jess asked.

"Monday. But that's if he can get somebody to take him down there. His dad has to work and his mom is supposed to go see his sister to do some wedding stuff."

Scott was a font of information on Will, that was for sure.

"Don't tell anyone what happened," Scott said dramatically.

"We won't," Jess said.

"Like your brother," Scott said and looked at me.

"I'm not going to say anything to anyone," I said.

Scott was starting to tick me off.

I swear, guys are such jerks sometimes.

Chapter Seventeen

"Guess what," Justin said to me as we came downstairs for dinner. It was the last free Friday night before football started and Mom had plans for a sit-down family dinner. Dad had made grilled steaks and we were supposed to eat on the deck.

"What?" I asked.

"Your boyfriend flunked his driving test today." Justin laughed. "I told you he was a loser."

"He's not my boyfriend. And how did you find out?"

"I've got the school wired. I know everything that happens there."

"You didn't say anything to him, did you?" I asked.

"If he's not your boyfriend what do you care?" Justin asked.

"Justin. Did you say anything to him?"

Justin flipped my hair, which he knew drove me crazy. "Don't worry," he said in a baby voice. "I didn't say anything to your cute little boyfriend."

"Good."

"I did announce it to the football team at the meeting we had after school."

"You are such a—jerk!" My teeth hurt because I was clenching them so hard.

"If he's not your boyfriend what difference does it make?"

"How would you like it if it happened to you?"

"It didn't happen to me. I'm too cool for something like that to happen."

I smacked him in the arm as we walked onto the deck. Not that he felt it or anything.

My mom gave us one of those looks of hers.

"Will you two quit fighting for one night?" she asked with her frustrated, "my children are driving me crazy" voice. When she talked like that it made it seem like we were trying to kill each other. Which might not be a bad idea since Justin was *such a jerk!*

"Yeah," my dad said as he speared a steak off the grill. "Let's all just try to get along."

He was laughing when he said it.

Ellie kept her eyes on him. As if my dad would drop a steak.

We all sat down at the umbrella table and started on our salads.

"I'm getting the sand delivered tomorrow," Dad said.

We all looked out at the pit that had been dug at the back of our yard. There was some PVC pipe stuck in it to hold the net. My very own beach volleyball court in my backyard! Too bad there wasn't a beach to go with it.

"It looks great, Dad," I said.

"Yeah," Justin said. "Just in time for you to work on your form . . . Grace."

"Justin," my mom said in her patient voice.

Justin ignored her. He'd been doing that a lot lately.

Dad looked at my eye. "That's a pretty good shiner you got going there. Just tell everyone you got in a fight and the other guy won."

"You mean the volleyball won," Justin said. "Everyone called her Spaulding at school today. It was like, hey Justin, we just met your sister Spaulding."

"Wah," I said.

My mom was starting to get that look on her face. The one that sends out a blinking red light that's sort of a countdown before an explosion.

I decided to butter a roll and concentrate on my dinner.

"And speaking of big dufuses," Justin said, giving me one of his smirks.

Obviously Justin wasn't paying attention to Mom. . . .

"Our second-string quarterback flunked his driver's test today."

"It happens all the time to kids," my dad said.

"It's lame," Justin said. "What kind of idiot sucks so much at driving that he flunks his test?"

"He doesn't suck at driving," I said. "He went through a yellow light is all."

"That is a hard call to make," my dad said. "Got to time it right."

"So why is it you know so much about it?" Justin asked.

"Scott told me at lunch," I said. "How did you find out?"

"Are you still eating lunch with that loser?" Justin asked.

"So what if I am?"

"Who are you talking about?" my mom asked. "Who's Scott?"

"Scott's the punter," my dad explained as he cut his steak.

"How did you find out about Will?" I asked Justin. "No one was supposed to know."

"Like I said, I know everything that goes on at school," Justin bragged.

"That doesn't mean you should announce it to the entire team," I said.

My mom put her fork down. "Justin. You didn't."

"Yes, he did," I said. "He announced it during the team meeting today."

"I did not," Justin said. Obviously he had noticed that Mom was getting mad.

"That's not what you said when we were coming down here," I said.

"Justin," my mom said in her patient voice. "Did you announce to the football team that Will had flunked his driver's test?"

Justin was thinking really hard about what he should say. It wasn't as if my mom and dad couldn't find out anyway.

Honesty was always best where my mom and dad were concerned.

"Everybody already knew," Justin said. I knew he

139

was trying to buy some time to squirm his way out of this one.

"I didn't ask if everybody already knew. I asked if you announced it to the football team."

"I might have mentioned it."

"Puh-leeze . . ." I said.

"Jenna," my mom warned.

Wait a minute. Justin is the one in trouble. It's not as if *I* did anything.

I took a bite of steak.

"Justin, I want you to apologize to Will," my mom said.

"I'm not going to apologize to that loser," Justin said. "You can't make me."

"Yes, I can," my mom went on. "You will call him and apologize. Then you will apologize to him in front of the team at practice on Monday."

Ha ha!

"Nope, not going to happen," Justin said.

"David?" my mom said.

"Hey, don't drag me into this," my dad said.

Uh oh. Division in the ranks. Justin knew it, too.

"I've got to maintain my leadership role on the team," Justin said. "It would be wimping out to apologize."

"It would be the right thing to do," my mom said. "The players would respect you more for admitting you were wrong."

"Mom."

Wow. Justin must have been practicing his dramatic voice.

"I can't." He took a bite of steak. "Can't we just forget about this? It's my last free Friday night. I don't want to have to worry about stuff like this tonight."

Geez. And he called me dramatic. Poor Justin. His Friday night party plans all ruined because my mom expected him to do the right thing. He might actually have to give up being a jerk.

"I am not happy about this," my mom said. She gave my dad one of her looks.

"I thought we were going to enjoy this family dinner," my dad said. "Didn't you say you'd made banana pudding for dessert?"

"Mom, you know how much I love your banana pudding," Justin said.

"Quit schmoozing me, Justin," my mom said. But she was smiling at him when she said it. He had charmed her right out of being mad with just one compliment.

I could not believe that he was going to get away with this. Poor Will had been humiliated in front of the entire football team and probably the entire school and it was all Justin's fault.

And just how did he find out about it? I thought only me, Jess, and Scott knew about it.

What if Will thought that I told Justin? I didn't even see Justin during the day, except at lunchtime.

What if Will was mad at me? He sure did act like he was at lunch and that was before he thought that I had told Justin.

"Aren't you hungry?" my dad asked.

I looked down at my plate. I had barely touched my

food, what with Justin and Mom fighting and then the realization that Will might be mad at me.

"I guess I'm not really hungry," I said.

My mom frowned again. She hated it when we wasted food.

"I'll eat it," Justin said. He speared my steak with his fork and dragged it onto his plate like he was doing me a big favor. Ellie watched the entire time, hoping that something would hit the deck. I knew Dad had been feeding her when Mom wasn't watching.

"May I be excused?" I asked my mom. Just the thought of watching Justin eat Mom's banana pudding was making me sick to my stomach.

And besides . . . I needed to talk to Will.

I went up to my room and signed on.

I saw Will's away message was up but I decided to give him a try.

Legolass: hey
KHQB17: out pulling splinters out of my behind.

Talk about depressing. Even his away message was a downer about football. I guess Justin must have gotten his way where Will was concerned.

Jess wasn't signed on so I decided to call her cell.

"Hey," she said. "Wassup?"

"The entire football team knows about Will flunking his driver's test."

I didn't even make it dramatic when I said it. I just said it.

"Bummer," Jess said. "What happened?"

"Justin announced it at the team meeting today," I said. "Jess, you didn't tell Justin about it, did you?"

"Oh—my—gosh. How could you even think such a thing? Besides, I don't even see Justin during the day, except when we're going into the cafeteria."

"Well, I didn't tell him and you didn't and that just leaves Scott, and since he's supposed to be Will's friend I don't think he would tell him. . . ."

"Hang on a minute," Jess said. "I'm going to check and see if Will is in his room."

"I just IM'd him and his away message is up."

"The house looks deserted. And the car is gone from the driveway."

"Maybe they went out to eat or something," I said.

"I'll see what I can find out from Scott," Jess said.

"Wait a minute," I said. "How are you going to find out something from Scott?"

"We've been talking some," Jess said.

I could tell she was smiling.

"Online, that is."

"Oh," I said. Why hadn't she told me that her and Scott were talking?

"Gottagotalktoyoulater," she said and hung up.

Geez. Jess and Scott were talking and she hadn't even mentioned it.

Or had she? Maybe I'd been so obsessed with my own problems that I hadn't really paid attention to what was going on with my own best friend. I mean I hadn't even told her how awesome she had played in the game. I'd been too busy worrying about my black eye to even compliment her. She had done really well. A lot better than me.

Or maybe she hadn't mentioned it. Maybe she was trying to figure Scott out, just like I was trying to figure Will out.

So what was there to figure out about Will?

I grabbed my pillow and curled up on my bed.

My first Friday night as a freshman in high school and I was sitting at home.

Geez. I thought these were supposed to be the best years of my life or something like that. So far high school had been one big . . .

"Are you feeling sick?" my mom asked from the doorway. She walked in and did the standard mom thing of putting her hand on my forehead. "Maybe we shouldn't have sent you to school today."

"Why does Justin act the way he does?" I asked.

"What way is that?" She sat down on the edge of my bed. Ellie padded in behind her and settled in the bean bag, which I'd pulled back out of my closet.

"You know. All guy-like."

My mom laughed.

"Mom," I said with my dramatic voice. "Why does he feel like he has to make Will look so bad all the time?" I rolled over on my stomach so she could rub my back. If she thought I was feeling sick then I might as well get a back rub out of it.

"Because he's frightened for his friend," my mom said as her hands made lazy circles on my back. "By making Will look bad he thinks that Ryan will look better by comparison."

"But what if Will really is better?"

"Then it doesn't matter what Justin does. Will will end up replacing Ryan and Justin will just wind up looking foolish."

"I think Will is better and that's why Justin is scared."

"Perhaps," my mom said. "And according to your dad, probably."

"So shouldn't you make Justin stop picking on Will?"

"If only it were that easy," my mom sighed. "I can't control how Justin acts when he's away from me, any more than I can control how you act." She looked over at my bent Legolas. I knew she was thinking about me sneaking into the movies. "All your father and I can do is give you guidelines and boundaries and hope that you remember them. I guess that's what growing up is all about. Realizing those things and living by them."

"So even if Justin is going to wind up looking like a big jerk then you're just going to let it happen."

"It's something that he's going to have to figure out for himself," she said. "However, I have told him that there will be no more announcements regarding anyone made at practice."

"I wish he'd apologize, too," I said. "And I wish I knew how he found out."

"And just how did you find out?" she asked.

"Well . . . I've had lunch with Will a few times."

"I bet Justin loves that."

"He's not the boss of me."

"No. But he is your protector. You know, the big brother thing?"

I made a face.

"Will is really nice, Mom. I mean *really* nice. And he's just moved here and he doesn't really know anyone and Justin is making sure that he doesn't have any friends."

"Sounds like he's got you for a friend."

"Yeah. Kinda."

"Is he hot?"

"Mommmm!"

Gross. Disgusting. Yuck.

"Yeah. Kinda. I guess." I rolled over on my side. "Jess said he's an elf."

"You mean like your friend over there in the corner?'

"Yeah. Like him. Only with short kind of curly brown hair and brown eyes."

"Sounds like Orlando to me."

"Yeah, I guess it does."

Mom kissed me on the forehead. "We're going to watch some DVDs later. Why don't you come down and join us."

"I will."

"The smell of popcorn will be your clue," she said as she walked to my door.

"Okay. And Mom?"

She turned around to look at me. I noticed her eyes were kind of soft and misty.

"Thanks," I said.

She smiled at me. "See you in a little bit."

I pulled my pillow close and thought about what she had said.

Did Will look like Orlando? Too bad none of my pics were around so I could compare. And the cardboard Legolas wasn't any help at all. Besides, his head looked a bit . . . lopsided.

Will was taller than Orlando. By about four inches. And his hair wasn't as curly, just kind of messy like he needed a haircut or didn't have time to comb it. It was close to the same color I guess. And they both had brown eyes. And nice smiles. But Will had a dimple. And his face was broader. Maybe it was because he was bigger all over. Not real muscley like Justin, but muscular. Lean. Fit. Because he was an athlete, I guess.

So no. Will did not look like Orlando. Not really.

Geez. It was almost as if I was obsessing over Will now instead of Orlando.

"Don't wait up," Justin gloated from the hallway. He was all dressed up to go out and he sounded like a herd of elephants as he went thundering down the stairs.

"Whatever," I said. "Don't hurt yourself flexing!" I yelled after him.

My first high school Friday night. I might as well do my homework. I got out my algebra and did the problems and then pulled my English textbook out to do the required reading.

So now I didn't have to worry about that any more. I smelled popcorn popping so I went downstairs with

Ellie right behind me and settled into our den for movie night. My dad had picked *Black Hawk Down*.

Oh great. I get to watch Orlando fall out of a helicopter with a really bad haircut.

But he's *sooo* cute. . . .

And I did like the movie. It was almost educational, stressing the futility of war. I know my dad really got into it.

It had just ended when the phone rang.

It was Justin. He'd gotten a speeding ticket.

Yes!

My big brother was finally in big trouble.

Chapter Eighteen

By Monday my eye looked a lot better. Most of the black was gone, nothing left but some green and yellow which actually kind of matched my eyes.

Hazel. Stupid name for a color.

I had IM'd Will at least a dozen times over the weekend. His away message stayed up the entire time and Jess told me at church on Sunday that she was pretty sure his family was out of town because the house had looked deserted all weekend. She also said that Scott was really ticked off about Justin telling the whole team about Will flunking his driver's test, but he hadn't talked to Will all weekend either. It sounded like Jess and Scott were getting to know each other pretty well. She was all "Scott this" and "Scott that" the entire service and she doodled his name on the bulletin and stuff.

Justin was in a really bad mood when we rode to school Monday morning. He was grounded and had to pay for the ticket, which meant he was going to have to work for my dad on Saturdays for quite a while. He'd also spent the weekend shoveling sand for my volleyball court in the backyard.

Yeah, he was crabby. But he couldn't complain about it because he did, after all, get a ticket. Sixty in a forty-five. I was actually surprised that he hadn't gotten clocked going faster. He'd probably charmed his way down.

At least he couldn't blame the ticket on Will. But knowing Justin he'd probably find a way.

"Are you going to apologize to Will?" I asked. It was probably a dumb move on my part to mention it, but I was still mad at him for what he'd done in spite of my conversation with Mom about how Justin had to learn from his mistakes.

And besides, Justin was already in a bad mood and I wouldn't see him for the rest of the day so I really had nothing to lose.

"Will, Will, Will," Justin said in a really bad and corny imitation of a girly voice. "You need to go back to your closet and look at your favorite fantasy man. Oh yeah, you can't. All your pictures are gone."

"You should apologize, Justin. What you did was just plain wrong."

"Are you practicing to be a nun or something?" Justin asked. "Or are you just the polite police?"

"I'm not the police," I said in my superior voice. "But I'm surprised you had to ask. I would think that after your experience on Friday night you'd know all about the police. They drive around in those cars with the blue lights on them."

"Shut up."

Oooh. Snappy comeback.

"So is your ticket a big secret?" I said. "Maybe I should announce it to the team."

"Go ahead. See if I care. Ryan was with me when I got it, so it's no big deal."

"You two are such idiots."

"At least we're not lame. Like your boyfriend."

"Shut up." Maybe I should work on my own snappy comebacks. "And Will is *not* my boyfriend."

Thank goodness we were at school, although the whiplash I got on the speed bumps made me wonder if maybe I should start riding the bus.

I looked around for Will as I walked across the parking lot. I was hoping maybe I'd see his mom dropping him off or something. Or maybe he'd gotten a ride with Jessica. There was no sign of him.

I did see Scott on the front steps of the school, but he ignored me.

Did he think I'd been the one who blabbed?

I really needed to talk to Will.

It was going to be a long time until lunch.

Jess had nothing to report when we met up for lunch. She didn't need to. I saw Will with Scott as soon as we walked into the cafeteria. I even ignored Justin as we walked in because I was concentrating on Will.

"Hey," I said.

"Hey," he said back. His eyes were darting around the cafeteria as if he was making sure no one saw us talking.

Then there was probably an hour of really uncomfortable silence. Okay, it was more like a few seconds but it felt like an hour.

"Um, did you go someplace this weekend?" I asked.

"Yeah," he said. "To my Grandma's, back in Kenton. Wedding stuff."

Wow. Kenton. I wondered if he had seen any of his old friends. He'd probably been all excited about going and getting to drive while he was there and stuff like that. And then he didn't get his license and on top of that Justin had embarrassed him in front of the entire team. I was kind of surprised that he even came back.

"I'm real sorry for what Justin did at practice on Friday," I said.

Will put up his hand to stop me. "No problemo," he said.

Geez, that sounded really lame.

Scott just looked at me.

"Can we talk?" I asked Will.

"I don't know," Scott said. "Can you?"

I made a face at him.

"Go ahead," Will said. He acted like he would rather ignore me. But it was kind of hard since I was right in front of him. "Talk away."

I gave Scott a look that I hoped would make him realize that I wanted to talk to Will alone. He just glared at me, so I jabbed Jessica with my elbow.

"Uh, I'm going to get something to eat," Jess said. "Come with me, Scott."

Okay, so she wasn't smooth about that kind of thing.

Scott glanced at Will, who shrugged his shoulders to show he didn't care what Scott did. Scott took off with Jess.

"Look," Will said. He ran his hand through his hair as he talked and the ends flipped up over his ears. "I'm going to take the test again in the morning, so it's no big deal."

"But Justin shouldn't have said anything." I stepped closer to him. It was kind of hard to hear with all the people talking in the cafeteria. And Will wasn't speaking in a normal voice. He acted kind of embarrassed or something.

"Don't worry about it. He's your brother. I know how it is." His brown eyes looked right over the top of my head.

"No, wait," I said. I was worried. I didn't like the way he was acting. And he wouldn't look at me. "I didn't tell him. I didn't even see Justin until after practice when he got home and he told me about you, er, uh . . ."

"I really think maybe we shouldn't talk anymore," he said like he wasn't even listening to me. "It pisses your brother off and it makes things hard on the team and stuff."

"Will," I said. I grabbed his arm. "I didn't tell Justin."

"Yeah, I know," he said. He stuck his hands in his pockets and looked down at his Nikes.

And I knew he didn't believe me. "But still, I've got to think about the team and I think it's best if we just kind of pretend like we don't know each other."

Now he was looking around the cafeteria. He was looking everywhere but at me.

And I didn't know if I wanted the floor to open up and swallow me. Or if I wanted to smack him.

Guys are such jerks.

My stomach twisted up into a knot. I felt the panic rising in my throat. I wanted to cry. I wanted to scream. I wanted to kick something.

And I was really finding it hard to breathe. I mean really hard.

And I couldn't show any of it because we were standing in the middle of the cafeteria and people were walking around us with trays full of food and I knew that if I did anything embarrassing I would never be able to show my face again at school.

"Uh, I guess I better get something to eat," he said. Actually he kind of mumbled it. If I hadn't been standing so close to him I wouldn't have heard him at all. And then he just walked away. Just like he didn't even know me.

You know how on TV sometimes you watch shows and things happen kind of in slow motion? That's how it was then. Everyone was moving around and yakking and eating and I could see them all doing it and it all looked kind of silly.

Worst of all, though, I could see Will walking away as if in slow-mo and there was nothing I could do to stop him. And I wanted to bawl at how unfair it all was.

And that's when I knew that I liked him. I mean I *really* liked him. A lot.

And he hated my guts.

And there wasn't anything I could do about it because he didn't want to talk to me.

Ever.

"What happened?"

I blinked.

Jess was standing in front of me with a tray full of food and Scott was coming up behind her.

"He hates me," I said.

"Noooo!" Jess said. "I had everything planned!"

"What?"

"Where's Will?" Scott said as he walked up with his tray.

"Getting some food," I said.

Geez, was that really my voice? It sounded kind of weird. Kind of far away.

"Are you all right?" Jess asked.

"Yeah," I said. "I'm not hungry. You go on. I'll see you in class."

Don't run. Don't run. Don't run. I kept repeating it over and over again until I got out of the cafeteria.

I walked down the hall and kept my eyes focused on the top of people's heads. I didn't want anyone to look at me. I didn't want anyone to see me. I didn't want anyone to talk to me.

I went into the bathroom. There were a bunch of girls standing in front of the mirror, combing their hair and putting on lip gloss and stuff.

I ignored them and went into a stall and slammed the door. Of course it wouldn't close. I guess I was lucky there was a door at all, considering it was a high school bathroom.

"Gosh," one of them said. "What's up with her?'

"Freshman," another one said and they all laughed.

Great. Now I was stuck inside the stall until they left.

And whoever had been in there last had forgot to flush. I tried not to look down at the disgusting mess of . . .

It was probably a good thing that I hadn't eaten anything for lunch.

I gagged.

Yuck.

I seriously considered throwing up.

Could my life get any worse?

Chapter Nineteen

Thursday. Game day. Our team was playing away today and Jess and I were sitting in the back row of the bus. It was a forty-five minute drive to the other school.

"At least he's got his license now," Jess said.

Yeah, we were talking about Will. He hadn't spoken to me all week. And every time I'd been online his away message was up. According to it he was still pulling splinters out of his behind.

"And the truck he's driving is really cool," Jess continued.

I just looked out the window. It was raining, one of those late summer afternoon thunderstorms that sneaks up on you when you least expect it. We'd all gotten soaked on our dash to the bus and all the older girls were worrying about their hair and makeup as if they were going to a party instead of going to play volleyball.

I didn't know if I wanted to talk about Will or hear about Will or even see Will. All I knew was that the days since Monday had been the longest and most miserable of my life. I had begged Justin to tell me who told him about Will flunking his driver's test and he wouldn't do it. I think he was actually pretty happy that Will and I weren't talking anymore.

But he had told me all about Justin's truck. He said it was a piece of crap, except the word he used started with an S instead of a C. I swear if Mom knew how he talked when he was away from home she'd have a cow.

Anyway, I had seen Will's truck when he drove in to school on Wednesday morning. A lot of guys on the football team had noticed too and had made a big deal about it which totally ticked off Justin and Ryan.

Scott had told Jessica that Will's parents had been hiding the truck from him at his uncle's house until he got his license. It wasn't new, but it looked really cool. It was silver and had big tires and one of those light bars across the top and was supposed to be four-wheel drive. It was an awesome truck. I think his parents probably got it for him to make up for him having such a hard time on the team.

I watched the rain beat on the window and imagined what it would be like to ride with Will in his truck with the windshield wipers beating and Maroon 5 on the CD player. We could ride to school together. Or maybe go to a movie together. Or just hang out together at the mall and get ice cream or something like that.

Except Will wasn't talking to me anymore. He thought I'd betrayed him to my brother and now he hated me.

And tomorrow night was the first football game of the year. Justin and my parents were really excited about it because we were playing last year's state champions and if we won then everyone would be paying attention to our team this year.

Except I'd be paying attention to the bench. Watching number seventeen pick up splinters.

Why did I have to fall for a guy that I had absolutely no chance with?

Of course, it wasn't like I had a chance with Orlando either.

Was it going to be my lot in life to love guys I could never have?

"So are you going to spend the night tomorrow?" Jess asked.

"Huh? Oh yeah, um sure, my mom said it was okay," I replied. "My parents'll be going out to eat with their friends if we win and will be in a bad mood if we lose so I don't want to have to hang around with them."

"Okay," Jess said. "I rented some movies and Hunter's spending the night at Daniel's house so we won't have to share the TV with him." She was excited because it was her first official day of not being grounded.

"Cool," I said.

I wonder what Will does after games. . . .

Jess was smiling real big and I looked at her.

"What?" I said.

"Nothing," she said. "Looks like we're here."

We had pulled into the parking lot behind a big gym. It was still raining and the noise on the bus got loud as everyone started moaning about having to make a dash through the rain.

I didn't care. I picked up the equipment bag and followed Jess off the bus. She ran for the door but I just dragged the bag along through the puddles. It was kind of heavy.

"You feeling okay?" Coach Miller asked. He grabbed the bag on the other side and held it up out of the water.

"Yes sir," I said.

"I don't think so," he said. "I think you're bummed out about something."

Now I was really glad it was raining. Because my cheeks were burning with embarrassment. If my dad knew that I was showing a bad attitude to the coach he would kill me.

But it wasn't as if I was going to get to play. Not after last week.

"What's up?" Coach Miller asked. "Are you mad at someone?"

"Er, sorta," I said.

"Good," he said. "Remember what I told you about getting mean?"

"Er, yes, sir."

"Today when you're playing, I want you to pretend that the volleyball is the person that you're mad at. And I want you to hit it as hard as you can over the net, right into the floor. That way you'll be getting back at whoever made you mad twice. Once when you hit the ball and the second time when it hits the floor . . . hard."

"Yes, sir," I said.

"Are you with me, Jenna?"

"Yes, sir," I said. "Er, Coach Miller? Does this mean you're going to put me in today?"

"Why wouldn't I?" he said. He held the door open. "Now let's go kick some butt!"

"Yes sir."

Wow. Get mean. Coach Miller wanted me to get mean.

"What was that all about?" Jess asked. She had been waiting for me inside.

"Just game stuff," I said. I was still thinking about getting mean but somehow all that came to my mind was an image of me lying face down on my bed kicking and screaming. That wasn't getting mean, that was throwing a baby temper tantrum.

We went through our warm-up drills and people started to come in for the game. Mostly parents for our side but my grandparents were there also. At least I didn't have to worry about making a fool out of myself in front of our student body.

The game started and I watched from the bench. We were playing pretty well but the other team was, too. Jess went in and served some and played the back row for a while. Coach Miller just left me on the bench for the first game, which we won.

I kept thinking about what he had said.

Get mean.

The second game was over. The other team won.

It was getting pretty intense on the court. Lots of kills going both ways. Lots of defensive blocks, and I mean the kind where you're protecting your body.

Get mean.

So what did Justin do when he was playing foot-ball? I knew that he got intense. I remembered when Will had knocked him down and then Justin had come back on the next play and nailed him.

You could tell all the way up in the stands when Justin was being intense. His entire body would get tense and then he'd get still and then he'd just ex-plode across the line.

So how was I supposed to do that?

Coach Miller said to imagine the ball was whomever I was mad at.

I was pretty mad at Justin. Mad enough to smack him, not that he'd feel it or anything.

But I could pretend that the ball was Justin.

Justin was such a jerk.

And Will was, too. He hadn't even let me apolo-gize and he still thought I was the one who blabbed and he wouldn't even listen to me when I tried to ex-plain it.

All guys are jerks.

"Jenna." Coach Miller pointed to me. "You're up."

It was the third game. We played best out of five. We needed to win this one. I went to the line to sub in.

"Let's go, Jenna!" my mom yelled.

"Be tough out there!" my dad yelled.

Be mean . . .

The other team was serving. I wiggled my fingers so they'd be loose. I didn't want to hit the ball and have it go flying off to the side or something.

Justin needs to quit being a jerk . . .

The ball whizzed over my head, one of those low flat serves that are really hard to defend.

Will should let me explain . . .

Jess was in the back. All she could do was get under it and bump it up.

Guys are such jerks . . .

The ball flew way up in the air and off to the side. One of the girls on the front line ran out and bumped it back in.

Another girl faked a spike.

And I jumped up and swung with all my might.

The ball smashed straight down, just clearing the net past a two-person block that the other team had thrown up. Another girl dove for it but it bounced right in front of her and flew off into the stands.

"Woo-hoo Jenna!" Gran screamed.

"That's my girl," my dad yelled. "That's my daughter!"

"Way to go!" my mom yelled.

I heard it all while my teammates high fived me and we huddled up because we were getting the serve. I was kind of shaking. I still couldn't believe that I hadn't screwed up.

I looked over at the bench and Coach Miller was clapping his hands and yelling.

"Way to be tough, Jenna! Way to get mean."

He really was pretty cute.

And I think I had figured out what he wanted.

I just pretended that the ball was a guy. Guys are jerks. I'm going to smack them by pretending that they're the ball. Maybe I should get an old volleyball

163

and draw Justin's face on it. Now that would tick him off big time.

I had a big grin on my face as I watched Jess rotate out.

"Let's go, Jenna!" she yelled as she sat down on the bench.

We served and it was high and deep so I knew they'd have a chance for a kill. My body tensed as I watched the ball get bumped toward their setter.

Justin is the ball. Justin is the ball. Justin is the ball.

I just kept thinking it over and over in my head, kind of like a little song.

The setter lofted the ball.

I moved toward the net with another girl on the team and we jumped up, just as their hitter tried for a kill.

Block!

Their striker tried to dig the ball out but it rolled off her hands and fell to the floor.

Score!

Hey, this was starting to be fun.

Justin is the ball.

Will is the ball.

We served again.

Will is the ball.

But I didn't want Will to be the ball.

We got an ace!

I didn't want to hurt Will.

I liked Will.

"Let's go, Jenna!" my mom yelled.

I figured I had better concentrate on the game.

Justin is the ball.

The serve was out.

I really liked Will.

So what was I going to do about it?

Our team huddled up while the other team got ready to serve.

"Way to play, Jenna," one of the older girls said.

"Thanks," I said.

It felt pretty cool, being part of the team. At least then you knew you were contributing something.

I went back to my place on the court and got ready for the serve.

The ball flew over the net.

It was out-of-bounds.

Our serve again.

Jess rotated in.

"Let's go!" I said as we lined up at the net.

We served and the other team dug it out.

Two hits.

Three.

I got ready but it went over my head to our back row.

Bump to Jess.

"Get ready!" she yelled.

Set.

I jumped up and swung.

Justin is the ball!

They blocked it.

I dove for the ball. I bumped it up, just as I hit the floor. I heard the crowd screaming as I landed but there was no time to see what they were screaming about.

Jess went running for it.

I jumped back to my feet.

She swung at it.

It was coming right at me.

I hit it backwards over my head.

It went over. I heard my dad yell something. There was so much noise I couldn't tell what he said.

Our team rolled back into position as the other team took their three hits.

"Block!" Coach Miller yelled.

I moved with my teammate to the net.

We went up together and blocked the ball. It rolled along the top of the net and then fell to the other side.

One of the opposing players tried to touch it and it bounced off her fingertips and landed, just inside the line.

"Point!" the referee said and pointed to our team.

"Game!" Coach Miller yelled.

We had won!

And I had played.

And not done anything stupid!

Wow. This was fun.

Coach Miller raised his hands and slapped mine when I put them up.

"Way to be tough!" he said. Then he leaned over so just I could hear him. "Feel better?"

"Yes sir!" I said.

I grabbed a drink and a towel as I sat down.

I could see my parents and my grandparents in the stands. My dad had a big cheesy grin on his face, the same one that he got when Justin did something awesome at a football game.

Wow. Too bad Justin wasn't here.

Wait a minute. I was mad at Justin.

But he was my brother. I knew he'd be proud of me.

Wouldn't it have been cool if we'd been playing at home instead of away and the entire football team had been here?

But I really only cared about a few people on the team. Well, actually one.

Will.

Maybe he would have congratulated me.

And then maybe he would talk to me and realize that it wasn't me who had blabbed.

And maybe Justin would quit being such a jerk and then Will wouldn't feel like it was hurting the team to talk to me.

Maybe I should just concentrate on the game.

Chapter Twenty

The first football game of the year. And the first football game of my high school years. Even though I had been coming to the high school games for the past two years to watch Justin play it felt different this time.

Now I was a freshman. Now I could sit with all the students on the other side of the band instead of with my parents. Now I was a part of things instead of just Justin Wheeler's little sister.

I rode to the game with my mom and dad. I had a bag stashed in the car because I was riding home with Jessica after the game to spend the night. Jessica's dad met us in the parking lot and put it in his van.

"Jessica's already inside," he told me. "And by the way, great game yesterday."

"Thank you sir," I said. Even though I had known him for years I was still kind of nervous around him since he was our minister.

Everyone was saying hi to my parents and some even congratulated me on the volleyball game.

I guess everyone had heard about my kills yesterday. Even though it had been an away game, the news had gotten around the school and lots of people had said nice things about my playing.

Except Will. Not even when I said "hey" to him in the cafeteria.

Yes. I had said hey to him. I had decided after the game last night that we needed to start talking to each other again. I had to find someway to convince him that I hadn't ratted him out to Justin. And I figured that the best way to get him to talk to me was to talk to him instead of pretending like he didn't exist, which was kind of hard since he was all I thought about now.

My mom would be thrilled that I was no longer obsessing over Orlando. I guess since my pics and stuff were gone I wasn't reminded of him all the time. I did still have my standee in the corner but it was wearing a straw cowboy hat now, which made the bend in the neck more wobbly.

Yeah, no more obsessing Orlando. Now all I did was wonder about Will. And in all that wondering I decided to say something to him. Like I mentioned, I walked right up to him in the cafeteria and said "hey."

And he looked really surprised when I said it.

And he said "hey" back.

And even added a "see ya later."

It was better than nothing.

I probably should have left it at that but I added a "good luck tonight," which really ticked Scott off. He said that since Will probably wasn't going to get to play that I should just drop it instead of rubbing it in.

I swear. Guys are absolute jerks. And stupid, too. Maybe my wishing him luck would get him into the game. Duh!

We ran into my grandparents as we got to the ticket gate.

"How's my girl?" my grandfather said and gave me a big hug. "Have you killed any volleyballs today?"

"Nope," I said. "Not today."

He pulled a twenty out of his pocket and handed it to me.

"Here, buy some popcorn."

"Thanks, Grandpa," I said and kissed his cheek.

Gran looped her arm through mine while we waited in line to get tickets.

"So, what color are your eyes today?" she asked.

I looked at hers and they were kind of green and sparkly.

"I'm not sure," I said. I mean I was all happy because I'd done well at volleyball yesterday and I was excited about the game because it would still be fun, but underneath it all I was kind of sad because of Will.

I just wished he'd believed me when I told him I hadn't blabbed to Justin. Then maybe we could work out the rest about Justin and the team and stuff. But unless he talked to me, then nothing would happen.

Gran looked at my eyes real close.

"I'd say more of a stormy gray tonight," she said. "What's got you down?"

Gee, she could tell I was sad just by looking at my eyes?

"I don't know," I said.

"Come on," she said. "Must be a guy."

"Well . . ."

I looked at my mom. It wasn't something that I really wanted to talk about. At least not yet. She wasn't paying attention to me and Gran, she was talking to some parents from the football team.

"Can I at least know who it is?" Gran whispered.

I looked towards the field where I could see the team warming up.

"Number seventeen," I said when I had spotted Will. He was out front with Ryan, leading the drills.

"Isn't that your number, too?"

"Yeah."

"Sounds like it's meant to be," she said. Then she brushed my hair back out of my face. "Don't worry kiddo, it will all work out."

"Yeah," I said. "I hope so."

We walked through the ticket gate. Jess was waiting for me inside.

"I gotta go," I said when she waved. "I'll see you later."

The weather was nice. Almost football weather. The rain we'd had the day before had cooled things down. I knew Justin was happy about it. It got pretty hot when you had to wear all that equipment. But at least it kept them warm when the end of October came around.

Jess and I had decided to wear our jeans with tank tops and flip-flops. We also had these cool ties for belts. We decided we looked good enough to hang out in the student section.

There were guys walking around without their shirts on that had letters painted on their chests. I assumed that when they sat together the letters spelled out "Panthers." Then there were a bunch of girls with T-shirts on that were painted with our school colors and different numbers of the players. I saw plenty wearing number twenty-four, which was Justin's number, and a lot with eight, which was Ryan's.

I swear, their heads were going to be so big by the time they graduated that they'd have to get those stupid cardboard hats that you wear with your gown custom made to fit them.

I didn't see anyone wearing seventeen, which was just fine with me.

"Maybe I should do that for Scott next week," Jess said. "Except I don't know what his number is."

"I think it's eighty-six," I said and pointed to the sidelines where Scott was kicking a ball into a portable soccer net.

"If Scott gets to kick then Will gets in, too, because he holds for Scott," Jess informed me like she'd been the one watching football all her life instead of me.

"Okay," I said. She was the authority on Scott now.

"Let's get some T-shirts this weekend and make some to wear next game," she went on.

And what number was I supposed to use? Justin was pretty much covered and since Will wasn't talking to me it would be foolish for me to wear seventeen. Plus, it would just be stupid since it was my number, too.

"Waddayathink?" Jess said. I realized that she'd been going on and on about paint and glitter and T-shirts while I was trying to figure out which number I should use. Maybe I should just go with Scott's.

"Sounds good," I said. After all, there was no reason for her to be miserable just because I was.

We walked by all the clubs and supporters that were selling T-shirts and pennants and spirit stuff and walked by the slushy wagon and the concession stand. The band was marching onto the field to play the anthem and the cheerleaders and our dance squad were all lined up on the track.

And back behind the goalposts I could see our team waiting to make their appearance.

Jess and I found seats just as the anthem started so we stood up again while the band played. Some people in the stands started giggling because they really weren't very good and some band parents were giving all of us in the student section dirty looks.

I just figured they needed to practice more. After all, it was only the first game of the year. They'd have it down by the time homecoming got here.

The cheerleaders and dance squad ran out onto the field carrying a big banner. I could see Justin in the front part of the team. He was jumping up and down. He was ready to play.

The announcer started yelling something about the Panthers. It was so loud you couldn't really hear it. Then the crowd started screaming and the team ran through the banner while a bunch of the cheerleaders did hand springs and the dance squad shook their pompoms.

"There's Scott!" Jess yelled as she jumped up and down.

I saw Will on the sidelines. It wasn't hard to find him, even without the number on his back. He had his helmet off and was standing next to the coach holding a clipboard.

Pretty obvious that he wasn't getting in. I looked toward the other end of the stands to see if I could find Will's dad. They were sitting with Jessica's parents. I guess they knew them best since they were neighbors. My mom and dad were sitting pretty close to them, too, but since Ryan's parents were sitting with them it had to make things weird.

Weird. Things had been pretty weird since school started. At least for me. I wondered if it had anything to do with all that maturity stuff my mom was always talking to me about.

It looked like we won the coin toss on the field. The other team was kicking off to our team. Our cheerleaders were lined up and doing a cheer. I don't think anyone was really paying attention to them except for their parents.

The dance squad had gone back to their place in the bleachers. They held their pompoms up and were shaking them while the band held this really long note waiting for the ball to be kicked.

It was as if everyone in the stands was holding their breath together.

The ball went flying toward the end zone. One of our guys waved his arm and caught it, then went to his knee.

"Why didn't he run?" Jessica asked.

"Coz he might not have made it to the twenty," I explained.

"Twenty?" she asked.

I showed her the lines on the field. "Ten, twenty, thirty," I said. "They get four chances to go ten yards. Each chance or play is called a down. When you get ten yards you get a first down and get to start all over again."

"Oh," she said.

I could tell we were going to have to watch some football on TV so she could figure it out. Or maybe we could just watch some of Justin's football movies like *Varsity Blues* or *The Replacements*. They were both full of hotties.

Ryan ran out onto the field with the offense and they lined up. Ryan took the snap and backed up to throw the ball. We watched as he stood there looking for someone to throw to. Meanwhile, one of the guys from the other team came around behind him and tackled him.

"Sack!" I said.

"Is that bad?" Jessica asked kind of sideways out of her mouth. I don't think she wanted anyone to know that she didn't have a clue about football.

"Yeah," I said. "We lost yards."

"Oh. But we get three more chances, right?"

"Yeah," I said.

They lined up again. This time Ryan handed the ball to one of the guys lined up behind him. The running back. He ran right into a crowd of defenders and they pushed him back to where he'd started.

I looked at the sidelines. Will was writing something on the clipboard while the coach was screaming at the field. My guess was he was screaming at Ryan.

The scoreboard said third down and 14 yards to go. They hadn't even played for two minutes yet. There was plenty of time. They were probably like the band, just nervous.

We were playing last year's State Champions, after all. And the way their fans were screaming you would think they were playing for another championship.

"He's going to have to throw it this time," I told Jess.

"Okay," she said. I really don't think she understood why, but she was paying attention.

They lined up again and Ryan took the snap. There was a guy close to the sidelines and he was open. He was practically by himself and was jumping up and down and waving at Ryan. Ryan threw the ball to him.

Or he tried to. The ball went into the ground about five yards in front of the guy. He tried to dive for it but it was just too low.

"I guess we're done for now?" Jess asked. "Or do we get another chance. It says four on the scoreboard."

"We have to kick it," I said. "Which means Scott gets to come in."

"And Will too?" she asked.

"No, coz he's punting. Scott has to catch it and kick it."

"Oh," she said. I could tell that she was really confused now, but she'd figure it out.

That is if we ever got close enough for Scott to kick a field goal.

Scott kicked the ball down field about forty yards and the other team downed the ball. Justin led the defense out onto the field.

"So now it's their turn?" Jess asked.

"Yeah," I said.

Justin was fired up. On the first play he practically jumped over their offensive linemen and took out the quarterback.

The crowd went nuts and Justin ran back to the line with his hands in the air. He wanted everyone to cheer and the crowd was happy to help out. The band played and the cheerleaders jumped around and the dance squad waved their pompoms.

"This is cool," Jess said as everyone stood.

The next play the quarterback handed the ball off to one of their running backs and Justin and another guy from our team took him out before he got past them.

The next play was an incomplete pass and it was their turn to punt.

"This could go on all night," Jess said.

"It's good defense on both sides," I said. I looked for Will. He was still next to the coach with a clipboard. It didn't look like he was going anywhere anytime soon.

Nobody did. The rest of the first half was just the same as the first few plays. Except that the other team did come close to getting a first down a few times.

But not us. We couldn't move the ball ten yards to save our lives. It was three quick plays and out and then the defense would take over. I knew the defense had to be getting tired. They'd played twice as much as the offense.

Jess and I went to check with our parents at half-time and Grandpa tried to give us some more money for the concession stand. My mom was talking to Will's mom. I wondered what they were talking about but didn't stick around to find out.

The band was marching around on the field but no one was paying attention to them except for the band parents. The dance squad did their thing and Jess and I talked to some people that we knew while all that was going on. Then it was time to start the second half.

We had to kick off to the other team and they ran it back the entire length of the field for a touchdown. After the extra point they had seven points on the board.

Everyone in the stands got kind of quiet. Especially when our offense came out and went three and out again.

And then the other team scored again. This time they kicked a field goal. They had figured out that they weren't going to get anything by Justin and were running their plays on the opposite side of where he was lined up. Justin couldn't cover both sides but he was still bothering them so they were forced to settle for three points instead of a touchdown.

So now it was 10-0 and the third quarter was ending. The other team had used up a lot of the clock on their last drive.

It was our turn to get the ball. Our guys lined up to receive the kick. We got a decent return on it and everyone cheered. It wasn't over yet.

Ryan went back out onto the field. I was hoping that maybe they'd send Will in because we were losing so he'd at least get a chance, but he didn't have his helmet on so it looked like his job was going to be official clipboard carrier for the rest of the year.

Ryan took the snap and it looked as if the entire team was after him.

"Blitz!" someone yelled.

Ryan went down under a pile of really big players.

And then he didn't get up when everyone finally climbed off of him.

Time was called and everyone was real quiet while the trainers and coaches ran out onto the field. I saw my mom standing next to Ryan's mom and dad, who both looked kind of worried.

"He's moving," someone said. That was good. I know my mom was always scared someone was going to get paralyzed for life or something when they played.

A couple of guys helped Ryan off the field and that was when we realized that he had fumbled the ball and the other team had recovered it.

"I think it's over now," I said to Jess. I looked at the clock. We had a little under ten minutes left and the other team had the ball. There was no way we could win. We probably wouldn't even score.

Our defense went back out onto the field. Justin was pumped up. They snapped the ball and he went tearing toward their quarterback. He plowed into him head first and the guy fell flat on his back. The ball rolled out of his hand and Justin jumped up and fell on it.

Everyone in the stands went nuts. They were screaming and jumping up and down. I could hear my dad above everyone else. He'd probably be hoarse tomorrow because he was screaming and yelling so loud.

Will put on his helmet.

"He's going in," I said.

The coach was talking to Will while the defense came off the field. I saw Will nod to the coach and then he ran out onto the field.

Justin was coming off the field and he grabbed Will's helmet by the face mask and said something to him.

I can't breathe.

I felt like throwing up. What did Justin say to him?

Surely Justin wouldn't want Will to screw up, would he? Wasn't the team more important than Ryan playing?

I was so nervous I couldn't stand it as I watched the team line up and Will take his position behind the center.

How could Will stand it? Was he scared? Was he nervous? What if he blew it? Not that he could do any worse than Ryan had. But if he did, it would be all his fault that we lost. He should probably just go ahead and pack up and move back to Kenton.

I really didn't want that to happen.

"Come on, Will!" I yelled as loud as I could.

"Yeah, Will," Jess yelled. "Let's go!" And then everyone else started yelling for Will, too.

I looked down on the sidelines and saw that Justin was yelling.

The ball was snapped. Will dropped back a few steps. Someone was coming for him. He moved out of the way and stuck his hand out and pushed the guy away. Right across the line one of our guys was open so Will threw him the ball. The guy took off with his head down and plowed through the defenders.

First down.

Everyone went nuts. It was our only first down of the night.

Ryan must be all right. I noticed that he had his helmet back on and was standing next to Justin. The coach came over and said something to him.

They wouldn't take Will out now, would they? Not after he had gotten us a first down.

I saw Will looking at the coach as he yelled something. Will nodded and then went back to the line.

This time they did the shotgun thing.

"He's going to pass," I told Jess. I grabbed on to her arm.

Will took the snap. One of our guys was running flat out down the sideline as hard as he could. Will threw the ball and it spiraled through the air. Everyone in the stands held their breath as it flew down field.

The receiver stretched out his arms. The ball landed right in his hands and he kept on running.

I pumped Jess's arm up and down as I screamed.

"Gooooooo!" I yelled.

Everyone around me was jumping and screaming. The referees put their arms up in the air just as our guy ran across the line.

Touchdown!

Will ran down field and the receiver guy ran out and they high fived each other with both hands.

Cool.

"There goes Scott," Jess said.

I wondered why they weren't going for two but I figured the coach knew better than I did. Will took the snap and put the ball down and Scott kicked it through the uprights. They ran off the field together and everyone slammed them on their backs or hit the tops of their helmets when they hit the sidelines.

There were five minutes left on the clock.

We had to get the ball back in a hurry.

But the other team knew that. And they were ahead. All they had to do was make a first down and they could use up all the time left.

The first play they ran the ball. The guy got a few yards before we brought him down.

The next play they did it again.

On the third down they were only one yard away from a first.

We had to hold them.

Justin was yelling at everyone on the defensive line. Then he pumped his arms. He wanted the crowd on their feet, which they already were. But he wanted it to get louder.

We all screamed like maniacs.

Their quarterback handed the ball off. Their guy charged toward our line.

And as a unit our team pushed him back.

They had to kick the ball.

There were just under three minutes left.

We could do it!

Ryan was going back in.

And the coach was talking to Will.

Then Will went in. What was going on? They couldn't have two quarterbacks, could they?

Our guys got in a huddle and then they lined up. Ryan went to the line and got on the end.

"Ryan's playing tight end," someone said.

"What's a tight end?" Jess asked.

"A receiver," I said.

Now I was really nervous.

What were they planning?

Will took the snap and did a short pass out to Ryan. He caught the ball but someone tackled him as soon as he did.

No yards but it was cool that he caught it.

Second and ten.

They lined up again.

This time Will threw it to a guy on the sidelines. He ran down the field a bit and got pushed out of bounds.

"Did we get a first down?" Jess asked.

I looked at the line markers. We were short.

The two-minute warning sounded. We needed a first down.

We got it the next time. Will kept the ball and ran it to the sidelines and stepped out of bounds on the other side of the marker to stop the clock.

We still needed to go about sixty yards in about a minute and a half.

"We need a pass," I said.

"Okay," Jess said. "Sounds good to me."

We lined up again.

Will dropped back to throw a pass.

And just as he drew his arm back one of the defenders grabbed it. The ball dropped. There was a mad scramble as everyone went for the ball.

Justin practically threw his helmet he was so mad.

The referees sorted out the pile. Will was on the bottom. And he had the ball.

One minute left. We had to call time-out.

I had to do something. We had to win. Even though Will was playing awesome, I knew that it wouldn't count unless we won. Especially since he had almost fumbled and lost the ball.

And the students were remembering that they were supposed to hate him after he almost fumbled the ball away. It would be a good excuse to hate him if we lost.

And then I remembered that Will had been there for me when I screwed up at the volleyball game. He had gotten up and made the crowd do the wave.

"Where are you going?" Jess asked.

"We're doing the wave," I said.

"We're what?"

I ran down to the front of the stands and started jumping up and down.

"Do the wave!" I yelled.

Everyone ignored me.

But then some people started to point at me.

"Yeah, let's wave," one of the cheerleaders said.

"We'll do it," a girl on the dance squad said.

I guess there were some benefits to being the coolest guy at school's sister. I was also cool, by default.

I ran down toward the parents section with my arms up in the air.

Some people did it. The band tried but they were playing. It stopped when I got to the parents.

"Come on!" I yelled.

I saw my mom grab my dad's arm and she pointed at me. My dad got a big grin on his face.

"We're going to do the wave, people," he said.

I ran back down to the student section and started again.

This time everyone did it.

I ran all the way down the stands and everyone waved.

I turned and looked and saw our team on the side-lines watching the wave.

Justin pointed at me and whooped as the offense lined up again.

I was out of breath so I watched the play from where the stands ended. It was closer to the end zone, too.

Will passed the ball to Ryan. Ryan took off running

down the sideline. There were guys chasing him. The clock was ticking. A guy tackled Ryan and he dove for the sideline to get out-of-bounds. He landed right in front of me. He was on the fifteen-yard line and there were thirty seconds left.

We had another first down.

They lined up again.

Will handed the ball off to a running back. He got about three yards and was tackled.

Will quickly turned to the referee and called the last time-out.

We were on the twelve-yard line. There were twelve seconds left on the clock. We were out of time-outs. We needed a touchdown.

They lined up again.

Will took the snap. He moved back three steps and looked for a receiver. Everyone was covered. A defender was coming for him. Will tucked the ball under his arms and against his chest and took off running. A defender tried to take him out and Will jumped over him as the guy dove for his feet. Another one reached for him and he curled his body away.

The seconds ticked down.

Five.

Four.

Three.

Two.

One.

Will dove over the line.

The referee signaled a touchdown!

We won!

Ryan hauled Will to his feet and beat on his back. Justin came running out onto the field and picked Will up. Will held the ball up over his head as Justin and Ryan and the rest of the team screamed and jumped around him.

And then Will pointed right at me. He had the ball in his hand and with the other he pointed at me and smiled.

I.

Can't.

Breathe.

Chapter Twenty-one

We won! The team was still celebrating after they did the handshake thing and ran off the field.

I couldn't believe it.

"We've got to go," Jess said.

I didn't even know she had come down to the track.

"My dad's got an emergency."

"We won!" I said.

"Yeah," she said. "My parents are waiting."

"We have to go now?" I said. "I was hoping we could hang around until the team came out so I could see . . . er . . . Justin and tell him congratulations."

"Mrs. Gladden's son was in a car accident and my dad has to go to the hospital."

"Mrs. Gladden has a son?"

"Yeah, the son is married and has a couple of kids, too."

"Oh."

I guess that was more important than waiting for Justin. It wasn't as if I couldn't call him later.

We made our way through the mob to the parking lot. Jess's mom and dad were already in the car and waiting for us.

"Would you two be okay on your own tonight?" Mrs. Gilbert asked. "I think I should go, too."

"Sure Mom, we'll be fine," Jess said. "It's not like I don't babysit by myself all the time."

"You know the rules," her dad said. "You . . ."

"I know, Dad," she said. "Don't worry about us. Just take care of Mrs. Gladden."

Wow. It must be pretty serious. They didn't even come into the house, they just popped the garage door opener and we went in while they backed out of the driveway.

Jess's house seemed really quiet after all the noise of the game. I dropped my bag in her room and kicked off my flip-flops. I tried to call Justin but he didn't pick up his phone. The entire team was probably out celebrating somewhere.

I took a peek out of Jess's window to see if there were any lights on next door. Will's room was dark but there was a light on downstairs. I knew my parents were out with all their friends. I wondered if maybe they had invited Will's parents to go along with them.

I smelled popcorn so I went downstairs. Jess had rented *The Princess Diaries* and of course the Harry Potter DVD's were out. She could watch those every day and not get tired of them.

We got cans of Diet Coke and settled in with our popcorn on the couch in her den. We decided to watch the game highlights on the news before we stuck in a movie.

"Did you call Justin?" Jess asked as we waited for the weather lady to finish with her predictions.

"He didn't answer," I said.

"Do you think Will and Scott are out celebrating with them?" she asked.

"I don't know," I said.

"Wouldn't it be cool if they were, since Will won the game?"

"Yeah, he did," I said. "That was so cool."

Outside we could hear the sound of a truck with those exhaust things that make them loud.

Jess ran to the window and looked out.

"What are you looking at?" I asked.

"Nothing," she said.

"Oh, here it is," I said.

Jess jumped onto the couch again and we watched as they showed game highlights and talked about how awesome my brother was and the great plays of our new star quarterback Will Addison. I felt like jumping up and down all over again in celebration.

"Isn't it great how they used Ryan, too?" I said as we watched the highlight of Ryan running down the field. "Maybe now Justin won't be such a pain to Will."

"I wonder where Hedwig is?" Jess said. Hedwig was her cat. She was big and white and fluffy, kind of like Harry Potter's owl, thus the name.

"I haven't seen her," I said. Hedwig was a lot like Ellie. Usually right where the people were.

"I bet Mom let her outside before we went to the game," Jess said. She went to the door that led to their deck. "Help me find her," she said.

I followed her out onto the deck.

"Here kitty, kitty," she said. "Hedwig, where are you?"

We heard a meow. But it was kind of a weird one. I'd never heard Hedwig meow like that before.

"Maybe she's stuck in a tree or something," I said.

"Come on," Jess said and went out into the yard.

It was kind of spooky. Jess had forgot to turn on the light and the trees at the back of their lot cast weird shadows over the yard. The grass was damp and cool against my bare feet and my toes curled up because I was afraid of stepping on something gross like poo or bugs or even a snake.

Then I heard this strange noise like someone running.

Jess squealed and the next thing I knew somebody picked me up and threw me over a shoulder.

I wanted to scream and I pushed myself up to do it but then I realized it was Will.

"What are you doing?" I asked. I was kind of out of breath because he had slammed me over his shoulder.

"Kidnapping you," he said. "We need to talk."

"Duh," I said as he put me down on the deck of his house. "Where's Jess?"

Will tilted his head toward Jess's house. "Scott kidnapped her. As a matter of fact they planned this entire thing so we would talk."

"They did? You mean me spending the night and Scott spending the night at your place?"

"Yeah."

His hair was kind of damp and wild around his ears and he was smiling and his eyes were all crinkly and shiny in the glow of the light that was on inside his house.

"So what do you want to talk about?" I asked. I crossed my arms over my stomach because it felt kind of fluttery.

"How stupid I am?" he said.

"Yeah, well?"

"Justin told me that he found out about me flunking my driver's test from a girl in his class that was there getting her license at the same time."

"She probably has a big crush on him and wanted to impress him by dissing you," I said.

"Yeah." Will ran his hand through his hair.

He did that a lot, I realized. Probably when he was nervous.

"Anyway, he also apologized for being such a jerk."

"My brother apologized? Wow."

"Yeah, I thought so too."

"He must have really been jazzed about the game," I said. "And by the way you were awesome."

"So were you," Will said.

"Me? What did I do?"

"The wave. A giant one."

"You saw that?" I'm pretty sure my face had turned several shades of red.

"Yeah, we all did. It was cool."

He put his hands on my shoulders.

"I'm pretty sure we would have lost without that wave," he said. "And I'm sorry I was such a jerk."

I looked up into his eyes. Yeah. Looked up. That was cool. Not like Orlando who was the exact same height. Up.

"You're a guy," I said. "You can't help it."

He laughed.

"I love your eyes," he said. "They change colors all the time."

"You do? What color are they now?"

"I can't tell." He leaned over.

"It's dark." He tilted his head sideways.

"I guess I'll have to get a closer look."

I blinked as he moved his head closer. And then his lips touched mine, gently, and then they moved a little bit, so I moved mine, even though I had never really kissed a guy before, and then he put his arms around me and I put my arms around his neck and closed my eyes and . . .

I—can't—breathe.

And I really didn't care if I ever did again. Why did I need to breathe when I was kissing Will?

I was kissing Will.

But more importantly, he was kissing me.

And for a first kiss it was pretty good. Not that I had anything to compare it with, but I had a great imagination. I had imagined it millions of time with Orlando. I had always worried about where I should put my nose and my hands and stuff, but all those worries had flown away as soon as his lips touched mine.

I guess that was a good thing.

193

And this was way better than imagining kissing a movie star who didn't even know you existed.

"Your eyes are hazel," he said when he finally stopped. He leaned his forehead against mine.

"Stupid name," I said.

"Beautiful color," he said.

And then he kissed me again.

Wow.

I could get used to doing this real fast.

Except that I heard Jessica squeal again. And then Scott started laughing.

"Hedwig!" she yelled and then Scott laughed some more.

"Will you get in trouble for being out here?" Will asked.

"Jessica's parents are gone," I said. "But they probably wouldn't like it."

"So do you think maybe I could come over and hang out at your house tomorrow or something?" he asked.

"Yeah," I said. "We could play volleyball. I've got a court in my backyard."

"Okay," he said. "But then we have to play football."

"Football?"

"Yeah, tackling and everything."

"You know that I've been playing football almost my entire life," I said.

"Yeah. I think that's one of the reasons I like you so much. You know the game."

He said he liked me. A lot. Or "so much," which means the same as a lot.

"Most girls don't understand it," he said.

"So how much do you know about volleyball?" I asked.

"My sister played," he said. "In college, too."

"I guess we've got a lot in common," I said.

"Yeah," he said. "But there is one thing."

"What?"

"Can you change your away message? Every time I see it I get jealous."

"You're jealous of Orlando Bloom?"

"Well, yeah, I guess. I mean it seemed like you were obsessed with him or something."

"I was," I said. "But I'm not anymore."

"You're not?"

"Nah," I said. "I grew out of it."

Epilogue

Justin screeched the Jeep to a jerking halt right in front of the church. I was sure everyone inside must have heard the noise we made as we pulled up.

"Do you have to drive like such a maniac?" I asked him. I pulled the visor down to check my hair and makeup. At least he had left the top up so I wouldn't get blown to death on the forty-five minute drive to Kenton, but I still had a serious case of whiplash.

"Hey, you're here, aren't you? And you're still alive."

"Barely," I said as I climbed out.

"Hey, Jenn," he said before I shut the door. "You look real pretty today."

"Thanks," I said and smiled at him. He went tearing off almost as soon as I shut the door.

I had on a flowery skirt that skimmed the top of my knees and a silky tank top with a sweater. I was even wearing heels. It was pretty warm for December and a really nice day for a wedding, even if it was winter and everything. I walked up the steps of the church.

Will was waiting right inside the door when I came in. I had been right. He looked great in a tux. He even had his hair slicked into shape, but I knew from experience that before the day was over it would be sticking up over his ears.

"Bride or groom?" he asked as he extended his arm.

"I'm a close personal friend of the bride's family," I said as I stuck my hand through the crook in his elbow.

"Oh really?" he said. "Lucky family."

He walked me down the aisle of his family church and I couldn't help imagining what it would be like to be walking down the aisle in a wedding dress and have Will standing in front of the church waiting for me. Reverend Gilbert would be there too, of course, since he was our pastor and Scott and Justin would be groomsmen, and Jessica would be my maid of honor. And maybe by then Will's sister would have some cute kids since she was getting married today and they could be our flower girl and ring bearer.

I could see it all very clearly in my mind as I slid into the pew and Will walked away to seat the next guest.

We'd been together since that night in August. We'd just had our three-month anniversary. Will had cheered my volleyball team on as we became conference champs and let me cry on his shoulder when we lost in the first round of state playoffs. I was there for him when the football team lost in the semifinals of the state playoffs. All the players were already making plans to go all the way next year and they were going to be attending a lot of camps and stuff over the summer to improve their game.

Justin, Will and Ryan all got along great now. Ryan had become a receiver but also played back-up quarterback, so that had worked out great.

Jessica and Scott were dating, too. At least they were now. They dated and broke up and then got back together only to break up again. It was getting kind of old since we never knew if they were going to be together or apart from one week to the next.

But most important of all, Will and I had worked out great. All my imaginings weren't as awesome as the real thing. Because it's not real until someone loves you back.

I also know that it's foolish to dream about marrying someone when you're only fourteen. Almost as foolish as dreaming about marrying a movie star. There's lots of time left before I have to make any life-long commitments. If it works out for me and Will, then it works out. If not, I'll never forget him because he was my first boyfriend.

But I really hope it works out.

Because I'm wild about Will.

Life, Love, and the
Pursuit of Hotties
Katie Maxwell
Author of *The Taming of the Dru*

Subject: Reasons Why My Life Sucks Right Now
From: Emster@seattlegrrl.com
To: Hollyberry@britsahoy.co.uk

1. The end of high school. You'd think that's good, right? Not for me.
2. Dorm life. It's going to take forever to hipify all those science and techno geeks in the Geek Dorm where I'll spend the next four years.
3. Dru's fantasy wedding. If she thinks I'm going to wear a pink-and-yellow plaid bridesmaid's dress, she's completely wacked out of her gourd.
4. Romantic graduation present cruise...without the nummiest boyfriend on the face of the earth? One word: *Waaaaaaaaah!*

A Bird, a Bloke, and a Boyfriend

Sally Odgers

A recipe for romance?

Take one bird. (That's Sarah, arm-wrestling champion extraordinaire.)

Add one bloke, who's known the bird forever. (That's A.J., who lives next door.)

Stir in one boyfriend—literally made to order. (That's Clay.)

Set the whole thing to rise in a tropical sun-soaked paradise called Pirates' Point, and what have you got?

That depends who you ask. Ask a simple question and you never get a straight answer from anyone....

MY ABNORMAL
LIFE
LEE McCLAIN

"But I'm not normal!"

Fifteen-year-old Rose Graham has never been to school. She's never had a date. She certainly never knew she was gorgeous. She's been too busy shoplifting food, keeping Social Services off her family's case, and taking care of her little sister.

Now, plunged into a foster family in affluent Linden Falls, she's supposed to act normal. But everything seems so trivial when all Rose wants is to get her family back together. At least she has the Altlives computer game to help her cope. And Brian Johnson's broad shoulders to drive her crazy....

- -

Didn't want this book to end?

There's more waiting at **www.smoochya.com**:

Win FREE books and makeup!
Read excerpts from other books!
Chat with the authors!
Horoscopes!
Quizzes!